R. W Gibbes

Cuba for Invalids

R. W Gibbes

Cuba for Invalids

ISBN/EAN: 9783337382261

Printed in Europe, USA, Canada, Australia, Japan

Cover: Foto ©Andreas Hilbeck / pixelio.de

More available books at **www.hansebooks.com**

CUBA FOR INVALIDS.

BY

R. W. GIBBES, M.D.,

COLUMBIA, S. C.

"Beautiful island! where the green
Which Nature wears was never seen
'Neath zone of Europe; where the hue
Of sea and heaven is such a blue
As England dreams not; where the night
Is all irradiate with the light
Of star-like moons, which hung on high,
Breathe and quiver in the sky."

NEW YORK:
W. A. TOWNSEND AND COMPANY,
NO. 46 WALKER STREET.

1860.

TO

WILLIAM SIDNEY SMITH, ESQ.,

Vice Consul of Her Britannic Majesty at Trinidad de Cuba.

My Dear Sir:

Accept my feeble acknowledgment of many obligations to you while enjoying an agreeable residence in your city. The restorative influences of her delightful climate I am sure were much assisted by the pleasure I received from your social friendship.

Very sincerely, yours,

ROBERT W. GIBBES.

COLUMBIA, S. C., Sept. 1, 1860.

INTRODUCTORY.

A severe illness from extensive pleurisy, terminating in effusion, having confined me to the house for four months, with very slow improvement of symptoms, I determined in January last to seek the reparative influence of a more equable climate. I left home feeble, out of breath upon the slightest exertion, and nervous, suffering at every change, and doubtful of more than temporary improvement. Upon reaching Havana, the uncomfortable feelings were greatly increased by the harshness of cold northers, and the variable climate of that city, too damp and depressing for northern constitutions. I was in the situation of an eminent statesman, who found he was obliged to ask himself the question, "where shall I go?" and had as much doubt in the reply. Whenever I, on enquiry, suggested any place, there was either total ignorance of it, or I was told of some objection—that there was no hotel, a very bad one, or exorbitant charges, or insalubrity and privations, rendering the locality uncomfortable or injurious—some difficulty existed in every case, and this I found influencing many to remain in Havana to secure present comfortable quarters without the risk of losing them by a change. In my embarrassment, I was relieved by the

B

advice of Mr. Crawford, the British Consul, who very
kindly informed me of the value of the climate of
Trinidad de Cuba, and urged my giving it a trial.

I went there intending to stay a week or two, and
found it so agreeable to my respiration and comfort
that I remained nearly five weeks, steadily improving
from the day of my arrival, and feeling at the end of
that time, that I was well enough to travel in other
parts of the island. I left Trinidad too early, and
subsequent experience satisfied me that it would have
been greatly to my advantage to have remained there
longer. I found pleasure in visiting other places, and
enjoyed beauty of scenery and sea air, but nowhere did
I find the softness and dryness and equability of
temperature of Trinidad.

During the few weeks I was there, the effusion in my
chest was removed as I gained strength and vital force,
and my gratitude to that sweet climate induces me to
recommend it to others. While absent I wrote light
sketches for the DAILY SOUTH CAROLINIAN, *currente
calamo*, which appear to have given pleasure and
interest to many friends, on whose urgency I have been
induced to put them in book form. Whatever I saw
was described under momentary impulse, and had I
re-written the letters, it would have no doubt been with
a labored and less attractive style. I therefore have
simply republished them, with some additional matter,
not because I consider them as deserving of more than
the ephemeral notice belonging to such composition,
but being desirous of giving my impressions of that

beautiful country, which I know I will be charged
with seeing *couleur de rose*, I risk the republication
as a means of communicating to a numerous class of
invalids my experience, which may be of service. If
a single invalid, induced to visit Cuba by my advice, is
relieved, I shall be fully reimbursed with the satisfaction of knowing that I have contributed to it. Life
is not to be valued by money, and health procura-
ble at any sacrifice is important. A visit to Cuba
costs money, but, as in my case, the interests of a
large family often depend upon such a change, and
a restoration to health fully repays the outlay. The
difficulty of finding a locality suitable to the case is the
chief source of anxiety in measures for relief. Believing that the south side of the island of Cuba
presents the strongest claims for consideration to the
invalid, whose nervous power is shattered and vital
forces diminished, I feel it a professional and social
duty to give my views of its value, based on personal
improvement. Patients requiring a change should
avoid the variable cold weather of the United States,
by an early retreat to Cuba about the first of November, and should remain upon the south side of the
island until the first of April. The chilliness of northers being then over, they may safely visit the northern
side, and enjoy the beautiful scenery of the trip from
Sagua to Matanzas, and revel in the enchanting view of
the Yumuri so exquisitely charming. A return to
Havana at that time will allow their visit to be more
appreciated, with improved strength, and I am sure

they will leave the island with greater satisfaction. For the temperature of Trinidad I refer to the registry of the thermometer, furnished by Dr. Urquiola, on p. 57. A comparison of its details will give to invalids suffering from affections injuriously influenced by the cold of winter, much to encourage them in the hope of amelioration of symptoms, if not full restoration to health. There is, probably, no climate presenting such attractive interest to them as that which I have recently enjoyed. He who seeks only pleasure in traveling, I hope will find my notes of service, in showing that there is much to interest him. The scientific man will collect abundant material for study, in the geology and natural history of the country, which will fully repay him for a visit.   R. W. G.

CONTENTS.

CHAPTER XVII.

CHAPTER XVIII.

CHAPTER XIX.

CUBA FOR INVALIDS.

CHAPTER I.

"Swiftly through the foamy sea
Shoots our vessel gallantly;
Still approaching as she flies
Warmer suns and brighter skies."

HAVANA, January 23, 1860.

As "time and tide wait for no man," the passengers by the good steamer Isabel at Charleston, were required to be "all aboard" on Wednesday night, so as to leave before day, and when they turned out, after the sun had risen next morning, they found themselves thirty miles at sea, and steaming along with a steady motion. The sea was calm, consequently the breakfast table full. About 12 m., we ran into the bay at Savannah, to receive a few passengers from a tug, and then our ship's course was resumed, keeping between the coast and the Gulf Stream. The weather

became cold and disagreeable, and confined invalids to the cabin, but twenty-four hours brought
a change of temperature, and overcoats even
were laid aside, and a delightful atmosphere enjoyed on deck.   No special incident occurred
during the voyage, our estimable captain knowing the reefs as well as the wreckers, and we
enjoyed the sight of green and blue and purple
water, approaching sometimes within pistol shot
of the reefs.   We passed quite near the iron
light-house on Carysfort reef, where four young
ladies, daughters of the keeper, reside with him,
where beaux rarely visit, their acquaintance
being limited to a few wreckers, who occasionally give them a call.   Robinson Crusoe's situation on his isle, we think, must have been far
more desirable than the isolation of these young
ladies in their solitary abode on the ocean.   This
residence is built of iron frame work, and is
firmly pinned into the coral rock.   The posts are
slender but strong, and the action of the waves
makes no impression on the small surface presented to their fury in a storm.

On Saturday, about 3 p. m., we entered the
harbor of Key West, where our captain very

kindly remained until 9 p. m., to give the citizens
the opportunity of enjoying the Campbell Minstrels, led by the gentlemanly and accomplished
Rumsey—his troupe being a portion of our ship's
company. The detention was no loss to us, as we
could not enter the port of Havana before the
morning gun from the Moro, and the arrangement
enabled us to arrive just in due season. Upon
passing the new fort, the minstrel band struck up
their fine music, and blew their own trumpets to
an anxious people. The island, *Cayo hueso*—the
rock of bone (coral?)—is about seven miles long
and half a mile wide, while the settlement does
not extend much beyond a mile. Here we saw
the beautiful cocoa-nut tree laden with fruit, some
of which regaled our company with its pleasant
milk and rich pulp,—also the tamarind and other
tropical fruits. In the unripe state the cocoa-nut
contains about a pint of agreeable fluid, and the
pulp is then so soft, that like cream, it is scraped
out and eaten with sugar. Most of our ladies
took a walk on shore, and saw the comfortable
and spacious houses of the citizens, who number
now about three thousand. On their return to
the boat, they brought a profusion of beautiful

flowers, among which were some magnificent roses. The absence of any public vehicle prevented our invalids enjoying the visit. The Government fortifications now in progress are very extensive, though we learn not so much so as those being built at the Tortugas, about sixty miles distant. While here our caterer procured some of the *King-fish*, which is called the salmon of the South,—resembling, as we think, our fresh water trout, and very fine indeed.

Invalids find good accommodation at a boarding house here, where, however, there is no great variety of fare, but those who enjoy fish and turtle will find good entertainment. The latter diet is very suitable for dyspeptics, though not formerly allowed. Nowadays rich animal diet is more appreciated than *soup maigre*.

We left the island at 9 p. m., the minstrels having put the folks all in good humor. We inquired what success was had, and were answered, "by the fall of some of the benches, a woman had a leg broke, and the people were delighted with the evening's performance." In our voyage to Key West, we coasted within the Gulf Stream, but now had to cross it, and during the night the vessel rolled very considerably. At 7 next morning, the heights of Cuba appeared, and at 8 o'clock we saw our signals on the Moro, as we entered the beautiful bay. At the distance of a few miles, the numerous white houses look like patches of snow, but as you near them, you find many of varied colors, of which yellow, blue and green seem to be favorites.

The scene as you enter the bay is enchanting; you can scarcely believe the exquisite picture is a reality. At the entrance, the rocky Moro lifts its craggy crest of brown stone high above you, with its guns ready to blow you out of the water, or rather into it, if you come with hostile intent; while the Punta stands on the left, with the fort of Principe to assist in exterminating the daring invader. On the summit of the rock, the light-house is placed, with a revolving light which can be seen at the distance of twenty-five miles. The entrance between the Moro and Punta castles is about 1500 yards wide,—its narrowest part about 350 yards. The depth of water is about eight fathoms. From the Moro, the fortifications of the Cabanos extend around the semicircle of the bay to the city, and present a most formidable appear-

ance.   Looking into the harbor, the tall shipping
at the wharves, with their slender masts, contrast
with the solid stone buildings, each one of which
presents the appearance of a fortification.   In the
beautiful harbor, crowded with ships and steamers, prominent are the Spanish men-of-war, several of which we noticed as sixty and eighty
gun ships.   They present a handsome appearance, and show their hundreds of guns, poking
their iron mouths out of the port-holes, ready for
filibusters.

Poco á poco we neared the city, and our
steamer steadily pressed on through the crowd of
ships and boats to her usual anchorage, and there
stopped to receive the visits of the Government
officers.   The favorite Isabel is always welcome
to the harbor.   First, a small steamer brought a
stern-visaged man, in blue frock and gold lace,
who received from the captain a bundle of papers,
after examining which he nodded to him, and
ordered his little steamer back to the shore.   Then
an individual in citizen's dress, with the most polite gesticulations, sat under the awning of his
boat and received another bundle of papers, with
the passports ; he then took his departure, and a

third official now approached and received the mails, after which the steps were opened to the friends of parties on board, runners of hotels, &c. Quite a difficulty existed in procuring rooms at the principal hotels, but finally we succeeded at the *Hotel Cubano*, kept by Mrs. Brewer, a lady well known to visitors from the States. Some of us who had a slight pretension to the Spanish language, were quite mystified at the distribution of a card *in English:*

"THE BOTH WORLD HOTEL.
Num. 80 San Ignacio Street
PLAZA VIEJA.

"In this establishment set as the European style receives lodgers which will find an splendid assistance so in eating as in habitation, therefore the master count with the elements necessary."

We regretted having engaged lodgings, as being without appetite, we needed "an splendid assistance in eating," which would have been quite an agreeable acquisition to an invalid.

We were soon surrounded by a crowd of small boats (guadaños) with awnings, to accommodate folks to go ashore, but a small steamer came alongside, to take passengers and trunks, which, after the transhipment, landed us on the Custom House wharf, where we came into custody of soldiers in seer-suckers, with muskets and sombreros. Our baggage was taken into a long room, and every trunk and carpet-bag was opened. The inspection by the officers was not very rigid, but enough to disarrange their contents, and disturb their smooth packing, if it did not ruffle the feelings of the ladies. Having passed the ordeal, each surrendered his passport, and paid $2 for a permit for thirty days to remain in "the ever faithful isle."

Our hotel agent took charge of baggage, and placed us by twos in the queer-looking *volante*, which carried us safely to the hotel. Although often described before, I venture to give you a description of it. Fancy two shafts fifteen feet long, with a pair of wheels six feet in diameter, and a sort of chaise-body capable of holding three persons at one end, and a pony mounted by a grown negro in gold or silver livery and long jack-boots at the other. The ends of the shafts reach the saddle, and the pony is kept in by long traces, and two straps over the back. The postillion or *calesero* has huge silver spurs and a long whip, which, as soon as you are seated, he plies freely, and away you go on a canter, soon dropping into a pace or trot. The wheels being high and the body low, with the horse six feet from it, it seems impossible to turn over, and the motion is easy and pleasant. You pay twenty cents to ride to any part of the city, the same for two as for one. The sight of these long lumbering vehicles, with the queerly-dressed negro postillion, is very odd, and their name is legion. The *quitrin* is a variety of *volante*, having a movable instead of a fixed top. The cost of these vehicles varies from $400 to $800, and even higher, according to the mountings, which are often of silver, and not mere plate. Occasionally you meet a buggy or carriage—some very handsome—but they are not numerous.

We were very agreeably surprised to find our hotel fitted up in handsome style, well carpeted, and with every accommodation of bedsteads and mattresses, while many have only cots and sacking to sleep upon; and we take pleasure in commending the *Hotel Cubano* as affording every accommodation to the invalid, by the kind and attentive hostess. The houses are built of stone, Mexican fashion, with an enclosed area at the entrance containing a fountain of water. Within the gateway or *porte cochere*, the only entrance you find, the *volante* is always kept. As you walk along the streets, you see the *volantes* in every large gate-way; and it is kept with more care, and certainly much cleaner, than the children of the family. Most of the houses, especially those in which shops are kept, are of one story, and the windows, extending to the ground, are without glass, and enclosed with long iron rods and bars, slightly projecting, forming a protection, as well as giving the opportunity to look out into the street. Being low to the ground, as you pass you can see the families within, usually sitting on rocking-chairs in lines on each side of the window, facing each other. In the evening the young ladies, dressed up finely, often take station at the grating, and receive the compliments of their friends in passing, many of whom they arrest and bring up to the bar to give an account of themselves. The ladies seldom go into the streets, and never alone, it being considered very indelicate to be without a gentleman—a party of four or five, however, may walk on the *Paseo* without attracting special notice. The American ladies, though, do as they please, and wear hats, while the Cuban ladies use only a veil or mantilla over their heads. Five of the afternoon is the fashionable hour for the senoras and senoritas to turn out in their stylish *volantes* on the *Paseo*, and at eight they go to the *Plaza de Armas* to hear music. They mostly remain lolling in their vehicles, but sometimes they deign to promenade in the *Plaza*. The ladies, also, do all their shopping in their *volantes*, requiring the clerks to bring out their goods to them.

Our impressions of the people and city will be contained in our next, *currente calamo*, as an invalid has no time to digest descriptions and sentences—he has enough to do to try to digest a diet which is new to him.

CHAPTER II.

THE DEEP.

" There 's beauty in the deep.—
The wave is bluer than the sky :
And though the light shine bright on high,
More softly do the sea-gems glow,
That sparkle in the depths below ;
The rainbow's tints are only made
When on the waters they are laid,
And sun and moon most sweetly shine
Upon the ocean's level brine.
There 's beauty in the deep."

TRINIDAD, (CUBA,) January 27, 1860.

On the arrival of the Isabel, among the visitors who came aboard, was Col. Wood, the Manager and Business Director of Donetti's Trained Monkeys. He told us that they were doing an immense business, the receipts being about $1,800 per day. He is said to have cleared upwards of $20,000 by this monkey-show. As we rode up in the *volante* from the Custom House, and met numbers of these queer vehicles, with the huge negro postillions in fantastic livery, gold and silver lace, blue and red jackets, with hat-bands of the same, and large boots with long, huge, silver spurs on, the latter sometimes on bare heels, we could not avoid the idea that Donetti might get large recruits for his show at any turn in the street. The *calesero* is a machine—his motions are mechanical—and you call to him to give directions at starting or in motion, he goes ahead heeding the notice, but turning his head neither to the right or left to give any sign of hearing you. We met numbers of negroes in long blue coats, trimmed with red and other colored facings and cuffs, with cocked hats and broad bands upon their heads, and these, we were told, were dressed to attend a funeral! In every direction some ludicrous object presents itself, and really when the bells for church struck up their tin-panning, it seemed as if the whole city was a burlesque affair. Had we arrived three weeks earlier we would have witnessed the amusing and grotesque exhibition of *el dia de los Reyes*, which would have increased the ludicrous idea. On that day (6th of January) the several tribes of negroes have holiday, and choose their kings—they dress up in every variety of queer and singular costume and character, and parade the streets in the enjoyment of their carnival. However, first impressions are not always the most correct.

The houses, all of stone, with iron bars to the tall windows, and jail-like looking doors, seem impregnable fortresses, and impress one in a despotic government with the idea of prisons being a large part of its polity, even in domestic and social life. These, with the espionage of crowds of soldiers with swords and muskets, at every corner, passports for coming or going, and posts with cannon all around, and the morning and evening guns of the military rule, give a fair specimen of a military despotism. No native of the island holds the most trivial office, or has any voice in public affairs—judges and magistrates and officers of all kinds, or their families, and even the troops, must be from the old country.*

Learning that the national sport of a bull fight is now only occasional, and that the citizens were to be entertained this afternoon, in company with a friend, we determined to attend at the *Plaza de*

---

* Since this was written, the new Captain General, in a liberal spirit, has given some minor offices to Cubans.

Toros. There were about a thousand persons present, though the seats of the circus open above, could have accommodated ten thousand. There were not over half a dozen ladies, and a few little girls in the crowd. At the sound of a trumpet in the upper gallery, the gates of the arena are thrown open, and a bull plunges in and runs around the circle, to all appearance excited by some means employed before he enters. Now come a few men in circus rider's costume, with colored flags, which they shake at him and run off, the bull sometimes pursuing the flag, and occasionally the man—who then runs to the side of the ring and jumps behind a sort of sentry-box, of which there are a dozen, and he is safe. Two *piqueros* (pike men) on miserable tackies with blinded eyes, follow the bull around, and with their long pikes endeavor to make him strike at the horses; but of five bulls which we saw, only one could be induced to gore the poor wretched animal before him—two or three times he struck at the rider, and came near unhorsing him. The *banderilleros* (banner men) failing to excite the bull, then stick into his neck a parcel of barbed arrows charged with crackers, the explosion of

which is calculated to enrage the worried animal;
and when they stir him up to run after the men
and the flags, great applause arises from the
audience.   If the bull cannot be induced to show
fight, as was the case with several, the crowd jeers
at him and calls loudly for him to be driven out.
But when he has been sufficiently chased by the
men with flags, or they have burnt out all their
crackers, the *matador* comes in with his long
sword, and holding a red flag before his face and
horns, as the bull attempts to pitch at him, he
dexterously thrusts his weapon into his neck, and,
when striking the spinal marrow, the poor beast
falls dead.   Out of four that we saw despatched,
the first lunge only killed one, and in several
cases there were four or five attempts before the
bull fell.   As soon as he falls, a sort of butcher
comes in with a knife, and gives him the *coup de
grace* in the spinal marrow, and he dies instantly.
The sport is shockingly cruel, and one in which
the sympathy of the audience ought to be with
the wretched animals. The excitement of the bull
is purely artificial, effected by goading, &c., there
being no savage wildness or native ferocity about
him, and he seems always watching to get out,

until goaded by the pikes or arrows. As soon as the bull is killed, two men come in, with three mules covered with ornaments and bells, and they hitch them to his horns and drag him off at full speed, to make way for another. They usually kill six bulls before the cruel entertainment is closed. A gentleman at our hotel informed us that he once saw two men and seven horses killed at one *funcion*—they were hauled out and the en· tertainment continued! The show is becoming less attended, and it is to be hoped will fall into such disrepute as to be abandoned soon. Formerly they had them once a week, now only occasionally.

The *Valla de Gallos*, or public cockpits, are situated in a large enclosure outside the walls. They consist of two amphitheatres, with benches around, a roof overhead, and a circular area in the middle. We however did not attend a cockfight, but for the benefit of our readers copy a graphic description from Dr. Wurdeman, p. 89.

"To see the cock-pit, one must devote to it the Sabbath, the chief day for the exhibition. As I passed along the road to it, I met many mounted monteros. Each had his long sword hanging

2

from his side, and a palm-basket under his arm, from which the head and neck of a game-cock protruded; the sides being gently pressed to his body, kept his wings closed, and secured him from being jolted by the horse's motion. It was already past twelve, the hour at which the sport commences, and as I passed through the gate, where stood a man collecting the entrance-money, I saw his table covered by the swords of those who had entered, the carrying any weapon into the pit being prohibited.

"Surrounding this, standing or seated on the amphitheatre of benches, a crowd of whites, mulattoes and blacks were assembled; all dressed in clean attire, and intermingled without distinction of color. In a box sat three judges, as dignified as if about to try one of their own species for life or death; while on the faces of the rest, each passing emotion of the mind was freely shown. Indeed, although I had visited all the hells of Paris—the gilded and licensed, as well as the obscure cellar in which the lowest did congregate—I had nowhere seen the inmost workings of the gambler's soul more fully exposed, than in the features of these spectators. Here, the warm sons of the South conceal none of the excitement the game produces; it is only modified by the temperament and education of each individual. The native of old Spain, his heart filled with the most perfect contempt of his creole neighbors, amid his dignified demeanor, shows by his gestures the interest he feels in the scene before him. The latter, with no such restraint, expresses his feelings as they rise, in varied gesticulations and vociferations; while Afric's dusky son, perhaps but recently brought out of his native forests, with all his untamed passions rife within, under the terrible feelings of the gambler, enacts the perfect maniac.

"Two birds were brought in, and having been weighed, their owners carried them around, bantering the spectators for bets, and occasionally permitting them to peck at each other. The sight of them, with the suddenness of an electric shock, seemed to rouse the latent passion in each bosom, and the place was immediately filled with tumultuous voices. Cries of offered bets resounded on all sides; '*una once* on the black, *una once;*' a shake of the finger from one opposite, and the bet was accepted, without a word having been exchanged. '*Tres onces por la plata;*' '*no! dos onces,*' answers one, who had only two doubloons; '*Tres onces,* make it up among your friends;' and some adding eighths, some quarters, the sum was completed, and a nod informed the better that his offer was accepted. '*Cinco pesos, cinco pesos por la plata,*' 'five dollars on the silver feathers,' cries a stout black, his body bent over the railing, his eyes protruded, and arm extended, shaking his forefinger at each person, to find one to accept his offer; '*cinco pesos, cinco pesos,*' he vociferates, in gestures and motion a perfect madman. Close by his side, another negro, intent on the same object, and anxious lest his rival should monopolize all the bets, with both arms extended, strives for the market by the force of his voice. Opposing banters from the backers of the other bird, in loud cries, are also heard, and the mingled voices in a continued din strike on the pained ear. One is surprised how accounts are kept, for no money is ever staked, and no witnesses called. A nod, or a shake of the finger, is the only pledge given, yet disputes never arise about it.

"The bets are now taken, the two birds are

pitted, and all but their owners retire without the enclosure. They commence fighting as soon as placed on the ground, and the now silent crowd, with outstretched necks, gaze intently on them. Not a sound is heard, but the blows given by the wings of the birds; but a lucky gash from the spur of one sets all voices again going, and odds are freely asked and taken. This was repeated several times, whenever one seemed to gain a decided advantage, until no doubt remained of the victor. The betters then looked on listlessly, as the triumphant bird followed closely his defeated adversary, which, now retreating, now attempting to ward off the blows, faintly and more faintly returned them, until completely exhausted he sank down, and unresistingly received the continued attacks of the other until life was extinct. The victor now exulted in loud crowings over the dead bird, but he was not permitted long to enjoy his triumph; for the owner, with his mouth filled with aguardiente, squirted the smarting fluid into his eyes and throat, and on all his wounds, sucking the whole bleeding head repeatedly. The combat lasted nearly a. half hour, for gaffs are not used; but no signs of

impatience were exhibited, and but little interest
was taken in the fate of the birds themselves,
independent of that of the bets connected with
theirs."

At present the Rumsey Troupe of Minstrels,
and the Monkey Show, are dividing with the
Grand Opera and Theatre the attention of the
Havaneros. There is also a large Circus Com-
pany here, for whom were brought over in the
Isabel some thirteen horses, the remains of
Yankee Robinson, who was sold out at Charleston.
The cost of bringing a horse from Charleston to
Havana is $40, and the duty $50, though for
breeding purposes they are passed free.

For two days the raw and disagreeable norther
has made us very uncomfortable, and, accompanied by showers, has confined us to the hotel.
Upon inquiry as to a pleasant retreat in the
country, we find that the hotel of *San Antonio*
has been abandoned, and that at *Guines* is a miserable affair, kept by a mulatto, and totally unfit
for invalids. Unless provided with letters to
private gentlemen in the country, the invalid has
no chance of any comfort, or even to find a place
to stop at. By the advice of a friend we deter-

mined to try the climate of the south side of the island—a longer way off than usually is visited—that of *Trinidad*, where there is said to be a soft, pure air, and pleasant temperature, and where northers are never felt, and a good hotel is kept.

At 6 next morning, we found the rail cars ready to start, a long train, and very much crowded. Our road branched off at *San Felipe*, and at 10 a. m., we arrived at *Batabano*, a shipping port, on the bay of Broa, some fifty miles from Havana. The country we passed through seemed mostly of vegetable gardens, though we saw groves of cocoa nuts, and fields of pine apples, with quantities of a species of palmetto. The stately palm towered above all, and seemed to shew an aristocratic influence of protection, scattered as it was over the fields.

> "Its feathery tufts like plumage rare;
> Its stem so high, so strange, so fair."

In some places there were groves of them, which are much valued, both on account of the wood for building, and the bark below the leaves for thatching—most of the farm houses being covered by it. The fruit, or nuts, called

palmiche, is used for feeding hogs, and is quite
an important article in that relation; a kind of
cabbage is found at the top of the tree, which is
boiled and much relished.

At *Batabano* we entered a fine large steamer
called *Rapido*, which goes to *Cienfuegos* and
Trinidad, arriving at the former at midnight, and
the latter next day to dinner. We had a cool
stateroom, the bottom of the berths being of open
straw, and a blanket the adjunct. A large company of Spaniards and Creoles occupied the upper
saloon deck with us, and a considerable sprinkling
of *Los Yanghees*, who are found everywhere.
Breakfast was served at 10½ a. m., and consisted
of a very great variety of meats—beef, mutton,
veal, ham, chickens, and fish of various sorts,
cooked in many disguises—and vegetables too
numerous to mention. You could get along very
well if you could find out what you were eating.
Breaded mutton chops made of pork—a very successful imitation—were very good, and rice was
properly cooked. Decanters of Catalan wine, or
Spanish claret, were abundant, and *Barsac*, or
Sauterne, at your call without extra charge, and
cafe-fuerte was handed round after the cloth was

removed. The Catalan wine has more body, is a stronger wine than French claret, and is usually drank diluted with an equal part of water. It is less liable to become acid, and agrees better with dyspeptics. It is universally drank in the island, and you meet with it every where. While at table, gentlemen lighted their segars, and were polite in offering them to strangers. Two of our ladies got into conversation with a Spanish youth who spoke English, and asking him some questions about cigarettos, he presented a paper of them to one, and refused to receive it again—such being a custom here, and it is considered ill manners to refuse any thing offered.

We steamed along the southern coast in sight of land during the whole voyage, and enjoyed a delightful gentle breeze, very soft and refreshing, after the ugly norther at Havana. The light peagreen of the water was very beautiful, and the loose, distinct clouds floating in the transparent sky, gave us pleasant ideas of a tropical region.

> "It is a goodly sight to see
> What Heaven has done for this delicious land!
> What fruits of fragrance blush on every tree!
> What goodly prospects o'er the hills expand!"

There was a company of soldiers on board—
yellow fellows, with seer-suckers and sombreros,
and marked by red cloth epaulets. They were
lying at ease in the forward part of the lower
deck, among negroes and fighting cocks and
horses. At a long table some were playing *mcnte*,
for small sums, with women, imitating the company in the upper saloon, where publicly the dons
were putting down doubloons on the cards, and
looking as cool and imperturbable when losing as
when winning. Among the employès on board
were several *coolies,* who seem to be used for
every purpose, and are active and intelligent.
There being no stewardess, the ladies had a coolie
boy as *fille de chambre,* who seemed to know his
duties. Dinner was similar to breakfast, only
more so—*mucho-fuerte*—large dishes of meat and
fish, and vegetables in abundance. After dinner,
the dessert consisted of preserves, guava, &c.,
cheese, a sort of pudding, and a variety of nuts;
after which cups were placed at each plate, and
waiters—one with hot *cafe-fuerte*, the other with
hot milk—followed each other, to give you the
proportion as you preferred it. Tea is carried up
to the saloon at 9 p. m., but it is a miserable

attempt. During the morning, pitchers of *orange-ade*, from sweet oranges, and *bora*, a sort of beer and water mixture, sweetened, are placed on the table for general use.

Our steamer landed at *Cienfuegos*, at 1 a. m., on Thursday, but we remained on board. On Friday, after a pleasant run alongside the mountains of Trinidad, from Cienfuegos to Trinidad, we reached the latter place at $3\frac{1}{2}$ p. m., having found a car at Casilda, its port, ready to receive us, from whence a ride of three miles brought us to the city, the cleanest we have seen in Cuba. It is built on the side of the mountain, and beautifully situated.

CHAPTER III.

" To regions where, in spite of sin and woe,
 Traces of Eden are still seen below;
 Where mountain, river, forest, field and grove,
 Remind him of his Maker's power and love."

TRINIDAD, January 28, 1860.

Cienfuegos is the most regularly built city in Cuba, being laid out at right angles. It is situated on the bay of *Jagua*, "the finest port in the world," as the Cubans say, having an area of fifty-six miles, and a very narrow but deep entrance, of course protected by a fort, Los Angeles. The city has about six thousand inhabitants, a school, a theatre, and a newspaper. It has wide streets, and about one thousand houses. The climate is very salubrious, and there is what is called a good hotel. It is quite a trading place, and here we met several more *Los Yanghees*, looking after sugar and molasses. It is about two hundred and twenty miles from Havana. Our steamer remained several hours, enabling passengers to visit the city.

A young lady from Philadelphia came in our steamer, to become a governess at an *ingenio*, or sugar plantation, of Mr. H., about sixteen miles off. He was quite delighted to meet her, but his countenance fell when he saw her huge trunk. He said, if there were two smaller ones, he could carry them on a horse, like panniers, as they do everything here; but one large heavy trunk could not be disposed of, as it would require a barrel of sugar to balance it, and this would be too heavy a load for a horse. After some difficulty, however, he found a schooner going within a short distance of his *ingenio*, and soon we noticed the trunk on a pile of sugar hogsheads *en route*. Travelers in Cuba, who expect to leave the railroad routes, should have such packages as can be disposed of on horseback, as that is the common mode of traveling. Mr. H., with true Spanish politeness, invited us to visit him, but his estate was too much out of the way, and we returned to the *Rapido*, for Trinidad, where we arrived to dinner at 5 p. m.

We have a fine hotel, in usual style, with quadrangular open area, and marble floors—the chambers have similar floors, and the cots have

sacking and no mattresses. The house is admirably situated, overlooking the grand *plaza de
armas*, which is smoothly paved, and filled with
enclosures of iron railing, containing the most
beautiful flowers. Roses are abundant and in
full bloom, and the banana tree loaded with fruit.
Cocca-nuts and palms, and a large variety of
beautiful tropical plants, are to us novel and
attractive. On Thursday and Sunday evenings,
the Regimental Band, of seventy performers, dis-
courses delightful music to the senoras and
senoritas, who favor the *plaza* with their presence. They play several pieces from some fine
opera—last night, from *Traviata*—then a waltz
and a country dance, the latter grandly stirring,
with the full band, and close with a grand
march, and retire. In all the principal cities and
towns of Cuba, this musical soirée is a public
institution; at Havana, they are held every
evening, amuse the people, and stimulate the
bands to perfect themselves in difficult pieces.
Nothing is more refreshing than to sit in the cool
plaza and enjoy

"Sounds and sweet airs that give delight and hurt not."

Invalids bear exposure to the soft night breeze with little risk of taking cold. We saw no one with a cold while at Trinidad.

Quite near us is the cathedral, whence the everlasting bells are constantly pealing forth. Day-dawn is ushered in with a sort of Fourth of July rapidity of chime, which awakens all new comers in the neighborhood, and every now and then they burst out with vehemence and beat furiously. This morning they poured forth so long and rapidly, that at 6 o'clock we walked out into our piazza, and found a constant succession of females, white and black, going to matins. They all wear shawls and veils, or *mantillas*, with which the bonnetless head is covered—the ladies every variety of lace, and the blacks whatever they can get. Among the passers were the young girls of a convent school, in white, hoopless, with white mantillas, and those of an ordinary school, in every variety of costume, some very rich, and most of them with fashionable crinoline. On their return they passed through the plaza, and the sight of the little girls, with richly variegated shawls, among the flowers, was very striking. At eight we went to the Cathedral, and there found a large crowd of ladies, with few men, but many black females, at mass. The devout behavior of the congregation, the rich tones of the organ, with the occasional intermission for the priest, and the chant following, were very impressive. When the service was concluded, the ladies came out, most of them followed by a boy or girl, with their mat and chair, which are always carried to the church, there being no seats on the marble floor. In this Cathedral is a picture of *Christ bearing the cross*—which is truly fine.

Trinidad is a beautiful city, built on the side near the base of Mount Vijia—forming quite an amphitheatre. It contains sixteen thousand inhabitants, and two thousand five hundred houses—built in the same style as those of Havana—of stone, with bow windows, protected by iron rods and bars, though we observed many with the grating of wood. Glass windows are scarcely known even in the cities. The rooms are 16 to 20 feet high, and full of large doors and windows, while the floors are of marble or tiles.

In 1852, the number of deaths was only

354, while there were 834 births, and 79 marriages. It is a very healthy place, no doubt owing much to its great cleanliness, though seldom swept but by rains, and its slope preventing any accumulation of water. Upon inquiry, we learn that the yellow fever in Summer is rare and slight. The atmosphere is soft and balmy, and very grateful to lungs that have been oppressed by the cold air of the North. The air is so genial and pleasant, and the temperature moderate, that we are surprised at there being so few invalids here. The hotel keepers in Havana are interested in preventing it, by informing visitors that Havana is a fair specimen of the climate of Cuba, which is a mistake. About three years ago, there were many from our Northern States.

The only house kept here is capable of being made a fine one, but at present there is no female chamber-maid in it, and the fare is not as well cooked as we would desire, but considered very fine for Cuba. To-day we dined well on lamb and green peas. One, however, can get eggs and rice, bread and potatoes, and will find green peas, corn, fried plantains, salsify and many

3

other eatable vegetables—the meats are usually too highly seasoned, and cooked with Spanish oil; and when you rise you have *cafe sin leche*, pure; but at breakfast you have *cafe au lait*, which is always good; after dinner it is given without milk. Fried plantains are very nice, and one may breakfast on them freely— they are very like our sweet potatoe when so cooked. Fruit is delightful, and oranges, bananas, guanavana, mamelles and cocoa-nuts abundant; as yet we have seen no others. The city is badly supplied with water, though they have it raised by an engine, but most of it is brought in jugs from the country, four of two gallons each on horseback, *at about a cent* a gallon; while fine springs of cool water are abundant in the mountains within a mile, needing only pipes and a reservoir to supply it abundantly. The people of Cuba, however, are inert and destitute of enterprise—caring for nothing but making money and spending it. The water however (limestone) is very good.

We see here, as in Havana, immense moving masses of green corn fodder, stalk and blades, in the street, looking like a stack in motion; upon nearing them, however, you discover a pony's head sticking out in front, and find him loaded with some 250 or 300 pounds, of what supplies daily food to all the horses and mules in the city—*Maloja*—which is dealt out in bundles by the *Malojero*. Vegetables and country produce, fruit and sugar-cane, and even beef and meats and coal, are brought on horses in panniers—so heavily loading the poor creatures that they walk as if foundered in the fore-legs; in addition to the heavy load, a big negro surmounting it.

By the kind aid of Wm. Sidney Smith, Esq., British Vice Consul, so well known from his sympathy with the ill-fated Lopez party, we visited the magnificent residence of old Mr. Baker, who, a native of Philadelphia,* has lived sixty years here. It is a most elegant establishment, built in the usual style of Spanish houses, marble and mahogany being the chief materials

---

* Sir John Becker, excellentissimo, has since died. In consequence of constant infringement on his estates by his neighbors, he purchased a title from the Spanish Government, which gave him the privilege of transferring to Spain any litigation which he had, where his chances of redress were better than in his location. He leaves some $4,000,000 worth of property to be contested for by two sets of children.

in its construction. The apartments are numerous and elegantly finished, many of the best
workmen from Europe and the United States
having been employed on it. The drawing-room
and ante-room are paved in mosaic, of pieces the
size of a ten cent piece, which occupied six years
in polishing down to the proper level. Even
the open area is paved with marble, as well as
the piazza around it, in the second story. The
house is elegantly furnished, and cost $400,000,
but like the buildings generally, is filthy in the
extreme, and looks as if it had not been cleaned
in many years. It is mournful to see such
neglect—but these people have great ideas of
building fine houses, and when built, they are
left to take care of themselves. They are as
inert as they can be, and the servants are much
worse. As we entered the *porte cochere*, or
vestibule, we met some of the small children,
in their usual costume, a pair of red shoes, and
nothing else. One of them, about three years
old, came up and shook hands with my friend,
and walked up stairs and took the hand of a
grown sister, conversing with us, who seemed to
consider him all right, and this in a magnificent

establishment of one of the richest men in the island! In the streets, at every turn, you meet nurses with children in similar costume. Water is considered *dangerous* in this climate, hence children are seldom washed, and ladies use a towel with *aguardiente* to rub their faces and necks with. If you ask in the country for a basin of water to wash your hands, they bring it warm, and with it a bottle of *aguardiente*, which is very cheap, costing about five cents.

We have in our hotel a distinguished photographist from New York, who has an elegant establishment in Broadway. He says the difficulties between the North and South have affected every branch of business so much, that he has been forced to come to Cuba for something to do. He made a lucky hit in taking the Captain General and his beautiful lady, and he is "going ahead" furiously. He has a room in Havana, another here, and has just sent two of his men to open one at Cienfuegos. He has five artists finishing up his pictures at this place, and subjects are coming in rapidly. Colored photographs have never been taken here before, and the population being a rich one, our friend will draw a crowd, and while drawing them out, will draw in the *onces*, which are abundant among the wealthy creoles. We dropped in to-day at his room and found him taking the newly arrived Governor of this department, who was in full rig. The pictures of life size are very fine, but would be to us dolorously dear at ten ounces.

The officials have been "considerably exercised," in the last few days, at a reported victory of the Spanish army over the Moors, at Tetuan, and as they take every opportunity of magnifying the prowess of their great and invincible Government, the Governor authorized a brilliant demonstration at the theatre, last evening, in honor of the victory. Everybody had to go to show loyalty, hence the house was crowded. The Keller Troupe entertained the company with their superb *tableaux vivants*, and being close by, we ventured to look in upon *Columbus Landing in Cuba*, but the crowded house and densely suffocating smoke of segars gave us but little time to do more than notice the magnificent dresses of the senoras and senoritas, beyond anything we have seen elsewhere. The lustrous eyes, exquisitely penciled eye-brows in the beautiful foreheads, and the well formed busts, are very marked in the Spanish ladies. Their complexions are olive without any tinge of red— their stature fine models, and their hair jet black and exquisitely luxuriant, but we saw no really beautiful women among them. In the last act, when the attack upon the Moors was signalized, there were fifty soldiers on the stage, besides the acting troupe, and we learn that the cheering was immense, in proportion to the greatness of the achievement of Spanish valor. It is well the celebration took place before the full accounts of the battle are received, as it is probable the success of the Spanish army is only in the Government paper.

A subscription has just been started in support of the war, headed by the Captain General with $4,000, of his salary of $50,000. His pickings,. however, will soon make it up. If rumor be true that Concha received an ounce ($17) for each negro landed last year, that alone yielded $680,000.

Everybody is required to subscribe, as appears by the following circular issued by the Governor of Matanzas, a copy of which we accidentally procured:

"*Political Administration and Presidency of the Council and Committee for Subscriptions and Means for the War in Africa.*

"INHABITANTS OF MATANZAS:

"The illustrious Council of this city, and Committee for Subscriptions and Means for the War in Africa, established in this city by decree of the Supreme Government of the Island, have directed themselves to you, through me, with the sweet confidence that is inspired by a loyal and enlightened people, who has never failed to show its patriotic ardor and its enthusiasm for all that is noble and worthy.

"The Spanish Nation, to whom you belong, descended of the same race of men who twice, by their resistance to the advance of the Moslem, have proved the bulwark of civilization and of christianity in Europe, embraced with the sacred desire of maintaining that honor, which animated it amidst the smoking ruins of Zaragossa and those of Saguntus two thousand years before—

and of which the love burns brightly in the bosom of its sons—has embraced fervently the occasion to offer to her Majesty's Government resources to prosecute the war waged against the empire of Morocco to obtain the redress of repeated insults to the national honor.

"Inhabitants of Matanzas, the citizens of the capital of this rich and fertile Antilla, have emulously come forward with funds to second the noble impulse, the generous and ardent patriotism of our brethren in the Peninsula, and certainly you will not be the last to follow this glorious example, thus giving positive proof of your spirit of nationality and of the ardent desire you have, of contributing your share of the expenses of the bloody struggle already commenced by our valiant army, which, under the guidance of experienced and renowned chiefs, must obtain the triumph inseparable of all great and just causes.

Signed,

"The Governor, President of the Council.

PEDRO ESTEVAN.

"MATANZAS, 23d of January, 1860."

This address, with an accompanying printed circular, is forwarded to every inhabitant personally; fixing the amount of subscription equal to the yearly tax paid by each one, with as much more added as the ardent patriotism of each may suggest. The amount of the *positive proof*, in gold and silver, with any remarks one wishes to make, is written in the margin of the circular, which is to be returned, thus preventing mistakes which otherwise might occur. Mostly do we admire the forethought with which, fearing the Cubanos might possibly, in their ardor for their mother-land, be tempted to ruin themselves, the sagacious Council has kindly fixed the amount of their subscription. Please, gentlemen, walk up to the Captain's office and settle!

Fiestas are frequent; three days of the last week having been celebrated in honor of some saint. We attended one at a neat little chapel, on a hill, approached by a hundred feet of terraces. On each side of the way were seats of masonry, filled with the crowd of ladies mostly. Two priests passed, with long segars in their mouths, and we followed to the door of the church, as it was filled. The altar was beautifully illuminated with hundreds of candles, and soon the priests commenced a chant; after every few sentences, the fine orchestral band struck up, and played long pieces of exquisite music, occasionally assisted by the voices of many boys. The chief service was this fine music, excepting that whenever it ceased, the three bells were rung with great vehemence. As the service was closed, the band struck up a lively tune, very like a country dance, and the people retired, amidst the firing of crackers and fire-works. Next day was another holiday, and the tongues of the bells were in motion all day.

In reply to an enquiry of a Cuban friend, as to the name of this chapel, he writes:

"The name of the 'church' is *Nuestra Senora de la Candelaria de la Popa!* '*Popa*' signifies stern, and as *Nuestra Senora, &c.*, is located on such a commanding position in the rear of the town, you will perceive that it is by no means inappropriately named. Of course you are aware that we have a Saint for every day in the calendar, and sometimes half-a-dozen; at Havana, they have instituted two new ones, which are unknown elsewhere. In the church of St. Augustine there are two Virgin Marys, one is white, the other is of a mulatto color. At Regla, the Madonna is black—once a year the latter is carried in state through the town, attended by the Admiral and all the officers of the fleet, which is placed under her especial protection. Her last appearance was extremely grand; she wore a tunic of very rich silver brocade, trimmed with white ostrich feathers, her train was of crimson velvet, edged with gold lace, whilst her brow was enriched by a magnificent tiara of pearls and diamonds, which produced a very brilliant effect as they glistened in the sun; the *tout ensemble* would have been really elegant, but for her *crinoline*, which had been so carelessly put on as to cause people to make remarks! Amidst the roar of cannon from the Spanish ships-of-war, at anchor in the harbor, the enlivening strains of military music, and attended by the elite of the city, with an escort of half a regiment of soldiers, her black Saintship was promenaded through the streets of the city, which were strewn with branches of palm leaves, of flowers, and filled with thousands of kneeling devotees, dressed in their gayest apparel!"

Cock-fights are here as popular as in Havana, and as frequent.

CHAPTER IV.

"The breath of ocean wanders thro' their vales,
In morning breezes and in evening gales.
Earth from her lap perennial verdure pours,
Ambrosial fruits and amarynthine flowers.
Over wild mountains and luxuriant plains,
Nature in all the pomp of beauty reigns."

TRINIDAD DE CUBA, February 4, 1860.
The country around Trinidad presents as beautiful scenery as can be found on the island.
Less than a mile from the city, is the country-
seat, or *quinta*, or Senor Justo Cantero, one
of the wealthiest citizens, who owns sugar
estates, *ingenios*, and much property in the city.
His excellent lady is widely known for her
extensive charities to the poor. We procured a
volante for a ride before breakfast, and visited
this picturesque residence. The entrance is
through an immense iron gate, and the avenue
is lined with the stately palm and alame, alternating. The house is a modification of a city

house—a sort of *cottage ornee*, with a large veranda in front. At the back, the whole extent to the river, some sixty or seventy yards, is covered by immense bamboos, planted at the sides and meeting above, which, with their leaves, shade the surface, where a table remains, at which 380 persons recently dined with the Captain General. The house is handsomely furnished, and one of the rooms—fitted up for the Condesa Serrano, the beautiful wife of the Captain General—has the ornamental artificial roses still all over its walls. Several well-executed oil paintings, of the proprietor's *ingenios*, are hanging in the parlor, with a number of beautiful colored engravings in other rooms and out in the veranda. The garden is filled with every variety of tree of the island—the immense ceyba, the beautiful mango, filled with small fruit, the almond tree, lignum vitæ, with quantities of cocoa-nuts, palms and oranges. The rich banana and the fragrant pine apple attract your notice, with flowers of every description in full bloom. At a short distance from the house, a small river runs, of water as clear as crystal, about four feet deep, and you descend to it by stone steps from the bathing-house on the bank— the whole shaded by the immense bamboos, previously noticed. So cool and delightful a retreat from the sun has advantages and attractions in this climate that render it a most grateful refuge. The garden is in bad order, and seems not to be as properly cared for as it should be, and the roses and plants are destroyed most extensively by a large red ant, (*bibe agua*,) which we saw in myriads. The orange trees are also suffering seriously from the ravages of an insect which is ruining them. Among the trees, we were shown that which produces the forbidden fruit, *Toronja*, and had fine specimens of the fruit, which is not much valued, though when fresh it is juicy and pleasant. Beautiful walks among the various groves, are ornamented with *jets d'eaux* and fountains, handsomely arranged, and shell grottoes are met in the densely shaded shrubbery.

"Groves whose rich trees wept odorous gums and balm,
  Others whose fruit, burnished with golden rind,
  Hung amiable, Hesperian fables true,
  If true, here only, and of delicious taste."

Having amused ourselves sufficiently in this fine retreat, we entered the volante and drove about two miles to the *quinta* of a brother of Senor Cantero. Here we found another pretty place, with bathing-house and stream, and groves of fine trees and flowers in bloom. The Senora very kindly showed us around, and when about to leave, she sent her son with two large goblets to a cow tied not far off, and he filled them in our presence with fresh milk, which he promptly presented, smoking and foaming. Having bid *adios* and *mil garcias*, we resumed our vehicle and returned to the city, in time for breakfast at the usual hour of $10\frac{1}{2}$ a. m.

We did not mention the custom in Havana and other cities of driving the cow around to serve customers with pure milk taken from her at their doors. It strikes strangers very oddly to see it in the streets.

We walk usually before breakfast and after dinner, and lie about the marble halls during the day, reading, writing, and enjoying bananas and oranges, with the sweet breeze, which is seldom absent. The climate disposes to *siestas*, which

4

come in generally about 1 o'clock, as dinner is not ready until 5 o'clock.

Ballou, in a Cuban reverie, says:

"There seems to be, at times, a strange narcotic influence in the atmosphere of the island, more especially inland, where the visitor is partially or wholly removed from the winds that usually blow from the Gulf in the after part of the day. So potent has the writer felt this influence, that at first it was supposed to be the effect of some powerful plant that might abound upon the plantations; but careful enquiry satisfied him that this dreamy somnolence, this delightful sense of ease and indolent luxuriance of feeling, was solely attributable to the natural effect of the soft climate of Cuba. By gently yielding to this influence, one seems to dream while waking; and while the sense of hearing is diminished, that of the olfactories appears to be increased, and pleasurable odors float upon every passing zephyr. One feels at peace with all nature, and a sense of voluptuous ease overspreads the body."

This afternoon, we walked to the cemetery,

which is now a neat grave yard, within brick
and plastered walls, with quite a pretty little
chapel for religious services. The enclosure is
partly occupied with vaults, about seven feet by
five, ten feet deep, and covered by a heavy
marble slab, with rings, with the name of the
owner upon it. They are very close together,
and in them coffins are placed, one upon another.
The remainder of the yard is used for graves of
those who cannot afford a vault. Bodies are
buried about three feet deep, and usually without
a coffin. They are allowed to remain nine
months, when the bones are taken up to make
way for others, and are thrown into an enclosure
in a corner—a sort of Golgotha—which we saw
filled with skulls and bones. The cemetery was
much neglected, and a miserable place, until the
worthy English Consul, W. Sidney Smith, Esq.,
took up the work of reformation, and by his
influence induced some attention to the care of
the dead, and to him is due the chapel and the
enclosing brick wall. The space being necessarily limited, however, and no burials allowed
elsewhere, the disgusting practice of removing
the bones is constantly required.

We have been much struck with the number of blind persons we meet in the street, and find that inflammation of the eyes runs its course very rapidly in this climate. The practice of painting the houses yellow, blue and green is said to have arisen from the unpleasant effect of the glare from white, which is now always avoided. The curious variety of colors often seen on a house, makes a very odd appearance, while it is, however, very picturesque. Some of the streets have fine trees along the side-walks, but it is not general, as it should be in such a climate.

CHAPTER V.

"Hast thou e'er seen a garden clad
   In all the robes that Eden had,
   Or vale o'erspread with streams and trees,
   A Paradise of mysteries ;
   Plains with green hills adorning them,
   Like jewels in a diadem?"

TRINIDAD DE CUBA, February 6, 1860.
The climate of Havana is not suitable for invalids from the North. In addition to the numerous causes of excitement in that gay city, the northers are very distressing to the lungs, and the charge of $4 per day to the pocket. Persons in ill health should seek the country air, and on the south side of the island, where northers are not felt. The difficulty of procuring accommodation is very great; at *San Antonio*, the hotel is closed; at *Guines*, it is a miserable affair; at *Cardenas*, tolerable; at *Sagua la Grande*, there is no house of entertainment.

Trinidad is somewhat distant from Havana, but you go in less than two days, being one night

in a first-rate steamer, with good state-rooms, and
a very fair table. You leave by the railroad on
Wednesday morning, at six o'clock, and reach
Batabano at ten, where you embark in the fine
steamer *Rapido*, formerly an East River packet.
Next day at 3 p. m. you reach Trinidad. The
city is beautifully situated on the side of a
mountain, and seldom without a delightful
breeze. The temperature is equable, and varies
from 73° to 80°. An engineer on the railroad
here gave me the following record: December 3,
73°; December 4, 73°; December 10, 73°; December 11, 70°; December 18, 67°—the coldest
day this winter. The sea is in front and the
mountains in the rear of the city—the slope
being nearly 400 feet to the sea; hence you have
either a mountain air or the sea breeze, which is
soft and genial, bearing on its bosom a delicious
languor, which we suppose is the *dolce far niente*
of the poet. Its soothing influence upon an
irritable system does more than medicine, because its medication is combined with lightness
of atmosphere, containing a reduced amount of
oxygen for the combustion which wears out life
in such cases.

The Hotel de la Grande Antilla, the only one here, is now, since the 1st inst., in the hands of Mons. Bernard, who had the reputation of keeping one of the finest houses in Havana. He has a cook of great celebrity, and the table is excellently served and attended. There are some privations in the house to Northern habits, but the host seems very desirous to have everything arranged to the satisfaction of his guests.

Trinidad is the cleanest city we have seen, being paved, and washed by every rain. It is entirely free from dust, and is remarkably quiet, except that the bells of the cathedral and churches remind one constantly of their services. On two evenings of the week, the military band plays, in the plazas, delightful music from the best operas; and there is always some amusement or other at the theatre for those who can enjoy them. Country seats or sugar plantations in the neighborhood may be visited, and the beautiful vegetation of the island seen to great advantage. To those who prefer the entire quiet of the country, an opportunity exists for accommodation at a *quinta,* two miles from town, which has just been rented to Mr. Cascelles for

a house for visitors. It is in a beautiful neighborhood, and has the luxury of a fine bath-house.
On the whole, we know no more desirable a
place for invalids to pass the cold months; and
finding great benefit and pleasure in its gentle
breezes and agreeable temperature, we cordially
recommend it to our friends who may visit
Cuba.

Having been deeply impressed with the equability and mild temperature of Trinidad, we
sought anxiously for recorded information of its
thermometrical character, and were fortunate in
meeting an old class-mate who pursued his
medical studies in Philadelphia, and has for
thirty years been a resident practitioner in Trinidad. He very kindly has furnished the following most valuable memorandum, supplying the
desideratum:

A SUMMARY

Of the Meteorological observations made at Trinidad
of Cuba, lat. n. 21° 42' 30"; long. w. of Greenwich,
80° 2' 30"; about three miles from the coast, at a
height, over the level of the sea, between 180 and 360
feet.

Thermometrical observations, two daily, at about sunrise, and at half-past two o'clock, p. m. A series of 13 years.

Barometrical observations, two daily, at about sunrise, and at ten o'clock, a. m. A series of 7 years.

The observations of the fall of rain are of a series of 11 years.

The observations of windy, rainy days, and days of thunder, a series of 13 years.

Thermometer, Fahrenheit.

Mean heat of the 13 years...............................80.1
Maximum 92
Minimum, only once.......................................56
Mean at sunrise..77.1
Mean at half-past 2 o'clock, p. m......................83.2

Mean, Maximum and Minimum, per month.

Months.	Mean.	Maximum.	Minimum.
January......................	75.1	87	56
February....................	75.7	86	58
March.......................	78.1	86	62
April	80.0	90	64
May.........................	82.2	91	72
June........................	83.1	91	74
July........................	83.7	92	75
August.....................	83.9	92	78
September	83.2	90	74
October....................	81.2	91	68
November..................	78.7	88	66
December..................	76.2	87	60

The greatest fall of temperature that I have observed was on the 16th August, 1844, between 2 and 3 o'clock, p. m., during a hail-storm.   The thermometer from 88, Fahrenheit, fell to 76, but rose again immediately.

Barometer.

Mean of 7 years............ ....29.683
Maximum 29.993
Minimum 29.409
Mean at sunrise...29.662
Mean at 10 o'clock, a. m...............................29.704

Mean, Maximum and Minimum, per month.

Months.	Mean.	Maximum.	Minimum
January......................	29.759	29.953	29.617
February.........	29.764	29.985	29.512
March......	29.732	29.945	29.522
April.......................	29.704	29.914	29.546
May..	29.668	29.783	29.515
June........................	29.683	29.833	29.569
July......................	29.708	29.869	29.567
August.........	29.693	29.859	29.409
September..................	29.651	29.865	29.480
October.....................	29.630	29.843	29.506
November	29.675	29.890	29.452
December	29.749	29.993	29.594

Rain.

Mean of a year in 11 years..................48.06 inches.
Maximum of a year..........................70.40   "
Minimum of a year...........................37.08   "

Mean, Maximum and Minimum, per month.

Months.	Mean.	Maximum.	Minimum.
January	0.951	... 3.696	... 0.043
February	1.197	... 4.005	... 0.002
March	1.738	... 7.826	... 0.012
April	2.033	... 4.059	... 0.007
May	4.846	... 11.295	... 1.942
June	7.382	... 13.593	... 1.829
July	4.969	... 7.175	... 2.040
August	7.787	... 20.067	... 3.231
September	7.261	... 16.766	... 3.030
October	6.905	... 14.915	... 3.019
November	2.397	... 8.817	... 0.190
December	0.602	... 2.015	... 0.000

The greatest fall of rain I ever saw, was on the 15th July, 1850. In 45 minutes it fell 3.295 inches.

The other falls of consideration were:

June 29th, 1849, in 45 minutes............1.953 inches.

August 21st, 1850, in 18 hours ....4.658 "

June 20th, 1851, in 24 hours...............5.399 "

August 20th, 1851, in 24 hours............8.391 "

October 5th, 1851, in 9 hours.............4.590 "

November 18th, 1852, in 24 hours.........5.741 "

August 30th, 1853, in 24 hours............5.908 "

January 1st, 1854, in 6 hours...............2.749 "

In the 13 years it rained 1,575 days, and it thundered 1,183 days—of these numbers correspond to—

Days of Rain.

January.........56	May.........159	September...210
February... 55	June.........215	October 188
March.........71	July.........198	November... 78
April 72	August......220	December.... 53

Days of Thunder.

January......... 7	May 107	September...196
February....... 6	June.........184	October......110
March..........22	July.........237	November... 14
April. 44	August......250	December.... 6

The maximum number of days of rain in one month, 23; of thunder, 25.

During 13 years the following winds blew fixedly for 24 or more hours:

Winds.

Months.	N.	N. E.	S.	S. E.	W.
January........	29	163	0	1	4
February......	19	111	4	0	4
March..........	12	31	15	0	3
April..........	0	16	15	2	9
May..........	0	10	16	2	9
June	0	18	13	2	0
July............	2	25	2	1	0
August.........	0	24	10	2	0
September	3	19	27	2	2

Months.	N.	N. E.	S.	S. E.	W.
October	20	78	11	7	8
November	40	123	3	2	3
December	57	169	1	0	1

The 13 years contain 4,748 days. Out of this number 45 were not observed.

1,150 is the sum of days of fixed winds.

3,553, the wind has made a round in every 24 hours, approximately in the following proportions:

Between the north and east, 14 hours; east and south, 3 hours; south and west, 5 hours; dead calm, 2 hours.

During the same period of 13 years I have been able to observe the upper currents the following times:

North	above,	south	below	1
North-east	"	south-west	"	4
North-east	"	south	"	9
North-west	"	north-east	"	2
South	"	north	"	14
South	"	north-east	"	103
South	"	north-west	"	5
South	"	east	"	10
South	"	west	"	5
South-east	"	north	"	6
South-east	"	north-east	"	20
South-west	"	north	"	6
South-west	"	north-east	"	9
South-west	"	north-west	"	3
South-west	"	south-east	"	3

West	above, north	below......................	3
West	" north-east	"	18
West	" south	"	3

J. M. URQUIOLA.

TRINIDAD, April 19th, 1860.

This record is particularly valuable for invalids, showing both equability of temperature and uniformity of atmosphere in dryness during the months most adapted for their residence here. The salubrity of Trinidad, as a winter residence, is comparable with that of any climate in the world.

Dr. Finlay, of Havana, gives the mean temperature of the hottest months, July and August, as 80° to 83°.

As a contrast to the summary of the temperature of Trinidad, we give the following from the last (seventeenth) Registration Report of Massachusetts as the temperature of Boston, as a Northern climate.

Medical men and invalids can make their own deductions from the data here given, as to the importance of change of residence in many diseases from a Northern climate, so cold and inhospitable to feeble lungs and shattered nervous systems.

Table exhibiting the Mean Temperature of the Air in Boston, in periods of ten years, during the last thirty-five years; by Robert Treat Paine, Esq., of Boston:

	1825-34	1835-44	1845-54	1855-59	35 years
January.....	27.32 ..	27.39 ..	28.82 ..	27.28 ..	27.76
February....	29.32 ..	26.73 ..	28.87 ..	28.32 ..	28.31
March	37.16 ..	35.16 ..	36.63 ..	35.00 ..	36.13
April.........	46.87 ..	46.07 ..	45.47 ..	44.99 ..	45.97
May..........	57.34 ..	56.12 ..	56.29 ..	54.33 ..	56.27
June.........	66.31 ..	65.79 ..	66.16 ..	65.32 ..	66.04
July	71.52 ..	71.60 ..	71.68 ..	71.01 ..	71.52
August......	69.43 ..	69.15 ..	69.20 ..	67.87 ..	69.06
September..	62.13 ..	61.86 ..	62.35 ..	62.52 ..	62.38
October.....	52.28 ..	50.32 ..	52.71 ..	52.42 ..	51.86
November...	41.06 ..	38.90 ..	43.38 ..	42.19 ..	41.26
December...	31.86 ..	29.52 ..	31.78 ..	31.51 ..	31.12

Mean temperature of the whole year, in thirty-five years, 49.06.

CHAPTER VI.

"I could a tale unfold, whose lightest word
Would harrow up thy soul!"

TRINIDAD DE CUBA, February 11, 1860.
We have said much of the delightful air and
temperature of this place—the pure, soft, fresh air
from the sea, which we have almost constantly—
the thermometer varying from 73° to 80°.
Dr. Urquiola, a physician of high character,
whose registry of the thermometer is given,
informed us that the coldest day, in thirty years'
experience, was in 1842, when once the thermometer stood at 56°. The nights now are cool,
and thick coats are needed in early morning for
comfort. The invalid who comes here will be
repaid in breath, if the fare is not so agreeable.
There are, however, all our vegetables, and many
others, and they are present at all times. It is a
great fish market; yet, strange to say, no one but
licensed fishermen are allowed to fish—the poor,

who could live upon fish, are not allowed to
catch them, and a single individual bought from
Government the monopoly of the market at Havana—he requiring all licensed fishermen to
bring every thing they catch to him. This is
a protective tariff, the most odious we ever
heard of.

The incessant tolling and ringing of bells remind us of the constant occupation of the priests.
Night before last, we heard the sound of music
approaching from a distance, and learning that it
was the *procession of the Host*, we went to see it.
It being for a wealthy colored person, some hundred negroes, each with a glass lantern, in double
file and open order, marched along the street, and
at the rear of the procession was a volante, containing the *padre*, followed by a band of music.
He had been to administer the last sacred rite of
the "*Oleo*," to a dying man, and was returning to
the church. As the procession passes, every one
in the street kneels, and every house-keeper at
night puts a lighted candle at her door. Just as
we are writing, six strokes of the cathedral bell,
twice repeated, announce the departure of the

5

dead from this life—for a female five is the allotted number.

We have heard many stories of robberies and murders on the island, which are less frequent than formerly, though in Havana and its neighborhood there is danger in being out late at night and alone. A friend has favored us with the translation of the confession of a robber, a few years since, which was given to him by the priest who attended him. It has never been published before, and is so fearful a record of crime that we think it worth recording:

"CONFESSION OF A CUBAN ROBBER.—In the year —, Francis Xavier Lazo, aged 23, was consigned to the criminal ward of the Hospital San Juan de Dios, in Havana, to receive surgical aid for a severe musket shot wound in the shoulder. A few nights after his arrival in the hospital, he was supposed to be dying, and a priest was hastily summoned, to administer the 'Oleo,' according to the rites of the Roman Catholic Church; but on feeling the prisoner's pulse, the priest declared that the man was under the influence of some narcotic, and proper remedies being used by a physician, the priest's opinion was fully confirmed. On removing Lazo to another bed, a letter, addressed to the Captain General, was found under his pillow, written just previous to his taking the dose of laudanum, with which he had intended to kill himself. It may be doubted if the annals of crime bear record of greater atrocities having been committed by any single individual than those confessed by Lazo in the following paper:

" *To His Excellency the Captain General.*

"SIR: Being on the point of death, I desire to make known to your Excellency the guilty acts which I have committed in this island, in order that the individuals now in prison, under suspicion of being the authors of these crimes perpetrated by myself, may not suffer unjustly, and also that by making a full confession of my misdeeds, I may be somewhat relieved of the load of sin which oppresses my soul:

"1st. I was imprisoned in the city of Cuba for a robbery committed in the town of Buaymo, where I stole some articles of great value, for which I was confined in a cell, from whence I made my escape to Puerto Principe, where, in

company with a colored man named Joaquin, I
broke into a jeweler's store, and carried away an
entire case of jewelry. It was taken from me,
on the road to las Funas, by a Commissary of
Police, from whom I made my escape, but soon
afterwards returned and robbed the same police
officer. In Sancti Espiritu, I committed a similar
robbery of jewelry, and the same night broke
into two other stores.

"I then went to Trinidad, and broke into the
house of an Englishman, and took about $4,000
worth of jewelry and property. I was arrested
upon suspicion, but made my escape, leaving in
the hands of the authorities a trunk of clothes
and a pass, which I obtained from the alcalde of
Sancti Espiritu, under the assumed name of
Prudencio Belet. In Matanzas, I robbed several
houses, from one of which I took an immense
amount of jewelry, but being pursued, I threw
the greater part away, behind the jail. I succeeded in escaping, but soon returned to that
city, where I perpetrated many atrocities. In
the village of Guanagos, I broke into the house
of a Viscaino, from whom I took a large sum of
money and other effects.

"In the village of Guanabacoa, I committed great excesses, and first among the number I killed a man on the hill called '*Joaquin.*' I also killed a Commissary of Police named Martinez, and a Lieut. de Taraco. In the city of Havana, in Andrade street, I murdered a police officer named Maranto and his wife. I had been sometime contemplating this crime, inasmuch as that Maranto was the most energetic police officer in the service of the Government, and the one who had been most active in his pursuit of me; but as he lived in an upper story, it was difficult to get at him; however, I availed myself of a frightful thunder-storm, with wind and rain, and with a ladder and instruments for forcing the windows, at midnight, I proceeded to the residence of Maranto and soon accomplished my purpose. I killed him and his wife as they lay in bed. The same night and in the same street, I killed an old man; and the next morning, I went to look at the body, as it lay stretched out at the gate of the jail for recognition. A day or two after, early in the morning, I killed a Frenchman in Campanilla street, outside the walls of the city. Near to the factory, (now the

Hospital Militar,) and also in the vicinity of the Barracoons, I have perpetrated great atrocities of the above nature.

"Near Matanzas, towards dark, at a place called *Ojo de Aqua*, I met a man, from whom I took a watch and a large sum of money, and then murdered him. On the road to *La Mocha*, I met a gentleman and lady, whom I ordered to stop; the gentleman made a move as if about to draw a pistol; but before he had time to use it, I shot him dead with my musket. I dragged the body into the bush; and after forcing the lady, I killed her also, to prevent discovery. I then fled from Matanzas, as a large reward was offered by the authorities, to take me dead or alive.

"I then went to *San Antonio*, where I perpetrated various excesses. Returning again to Havana, I broke into the house of the Captain of Artillery, Don Jose Solear, and carried off a large sum of money. I remained sometime in Havana, robbing, among others, the house of the merchant Vias. Compelled again to fly from Havana, I proceeded to Guanajas, where I was captured by the officer of the district, who caused me to be tightly bound with cords, and with an escort of fourteen men sent me to Havana; but at a stopping place on the way, I managed to get my hands loose, and seizing a machete, belonging to the chief of my guards, made an attempt to escape. I was hotly pursued by several of my captors, one of whom had severely wounded me by a musket shot in the shoulder, and finding myself about to fall from loss of blood, I turned round to meet my pursuers, killing the first one that came up, the chief, with his own sword. I was, however, soon overpowered and conveyed to this city; where I am now lying at the point of death, having swallowed a dose of laudanum.

"My strength is rapidly failing, and I have given your Excellency but an incomplete statement of the dreadful crimes which now so heavily weigh upon my soul. As well as I can remember, I have murdered, during my shameful career of sin and wickedness, upwards of twenty-three innocent people, whose blood cries out to Heaven against me.

"FRANCISCO XAVIER LAZO.
"Hospital of San Juan de Dios."

This miserable wretch recovered from the effects of the poison he had taken, and was publicly executed in front of the Punta Castle, acknowledging, in his last moments, that his death was but a poor atonement for the lives of the unfortunate victims who had fallen into his murderous hands.

CHAPTER VII.

" And there she lay without e'en a shroud,—
And strangers were around the coffinless;
Not a kinsman was seen among the crowd,—
Not an eye to weep, nor a lip to bless."

TRINIDAD DE CUBA, February 13, 1860. In our last letter from Havana, we mentioned seeing a large number of negroes, dressed in fancy coats, cocked hats, &c., for a funeral. We have since found that they were the hired mourners, furnished by the undertaker, who has on hand constantly a large stock of such livery, to supply any amount of demand. In proportion to the wealth, dignity and standing of citizens, is the number of such attendants, the expenses of a burial being enormous. Here in Trinidad an old gentleman, in moderate circumstances, recently lost his wife—the expenses of the funeral were $700. We saw a burial of an old lady, who had once owned a sugar estate, and was connected with some of the best families, but was now

poor; she was taken to the cemetery by four
negroes, and from the coffin was thrown into the
grave, three feet deep, and the earth piled upon
her. No service was held, and no persons attended, because she was poor! Such is life!

On yesterday, was High Mass in the Cathedral; after which was a solemn *Te Deum*, in
honor of the Queen's *accouchement*. Two priests
received the Governor and suite at the door,
sprinkling the way with holy water. The Governor was attended by his staff, all the officers
of the regiment in uniform, the corporation,
custom house officials, postmaster and other
Government officers. Upon their entering, the
ladies moved their mats and chairs, to make way
for them, and they arranged themselves in line
at the sides of the church. Each was then
furnished with a wax candle, three or four feet
long, which they held lighted during the whole
service. Five priests, in rich vestments, approached the altar and commenced the service,
alternating their chants with the music of the
band. The organ was not used, but a large band
of fine performers on many instruments played a
number of the choicest pieces from the best

operas. The music was very grand, and lasted about an hour.

In business matters, there seems to be no difference between Sundays and other days—the stores are all open, and things are hawked about the streets as during the week. Sunday is the great day for amusement—bull-fights and cock-fights, and balls being given on that day. Passing by the Theatre, last evening, on returning from a walk, an immense crowd induced an inquiry as to the cause of it, when we found that there was a "*dignity ball*" of colored folks going on. A man standing at the door had just communicated the information that the house was full, and no more could be admitted. At these balls, the colored ladies vie with their betters, though not recognizing them as such, and dress in the extreme of fashion. The colored gents have equal pretensions, and their style of dress is a prominent feature in the picture.

It appears that the Government, which is alive to taxes in every form, issued an order to the "cullud pussons" to have two balls and a grand masquerade, the profits to be applied to the fund for the war against the Moors. One dollar is the

entrance fee, and as there is no supper provided—
only the cost of the Theatre and music—the
balance, from such an immense crowd, must be
something considerable. The acting Governor
and suite attended, and remained until 1 a. m.,
promenading and enjoying the scene, while the
dark ladies and gentlemen went through the
various dances. We met, to-day, a friend who
was present, and he reports that the affair was
well conducted, with proper behavior on all sides.

Quite a commotion has been excited by the
new Governor having ordered the annual *Fiesta*
of the river Ay to be suppressed this year. It is
a great occasion, and is a sort of carnival on the
banks of the river, a few miles off. Everybody
goes, and the preparations and expenditures are
on a grand scale. It lasts four days, and dancing,
card playing and all sorts of amusements prevail;
they then move off to another river, and the
same gayety is repeated all through the district.
A new Governor, who has only been two months
here, was induced to believe, by some old lady
whose son had just lost heavily by gambling,
that it would do much to put down that vice, so
he recommended to the new Captain General the

suppression of the festival, and he approved it, and there has been great dissatisfaction; but in this Government there is no redress. A few days since an order came transferring the Governor to Puerto Principe, and the Governor of that city is to come here; meanwhile, the Colonel of the regiment, who is *locum tenens*, gives *dignity balls*, that he may strut his brief official existence as conspicuously as possible.

To keep the ball in motion, the Government paper at Havana gives notice of a grand "*funcion taurica*," or "bull-fight entertainment," ordered for Sunday, the 19th, at which the Condesa San Antonio, the lady of the Captain General, and other senoras and senoritas, will be present. Their boxes will be splendidly lined with magnificent silks and satins, and adorned with artificial flowers, &c. The bulls have been named *Tangier, Bullones, Tetuan, Serrallo, Renegado, Monte Negros and Marruecos*, and will be elegantly adorned. The death of these poor animals, with such names, by the sword, is to be a prefiguring of what the Moorish towns will receive from the attacks of Spanish valor. Before the acts of slaying the bulls, there will be a grand bayonet fencing match by soldiers, and no doubt there will be an immense concourse of the fashionables to enjoy these gentle sports.

The steamer Water Witch, one of our Government vessels cruising after slavers, is here. By invitation of her courteous Captain, Sartori, we went on board to visit the officers. She is the smallest craft in our navy, and her complement of men, including officers, is sixty-six. She carries three Dahlgren brass pieces, which no doubt will prove good speaking-trumpets to the slavers, if ever they can see them—but, like the *pulgas*, or fleas, you know they are there, but it is hard to put your finger on them. The vessel is very neat and clean, and everything in fine order, and the officers a capital set of gentlemen. They await the arrival of the Wyandotte to be relieved, and will then go to Pensacola to refit.*

---

* The activity of our cruisers in these waters is cause of great uneasiness to the slave traders, *who have been completely deceived in their calculations.* They were led to believe that the arrival of American cruisers to replace the " British " was the most favorable thing that could happen to them ; that the captain of an American man-of-war would on no account capture a vessel hoisting the American flag, and in fact that the arrival of the United States ships was altogether *a farce!* This explains

The ladies of our party were delighted with the visit; and enjoyed a most satisfactory lunch of good things in American style. The neat little cabin was a merry place on the occasion. We enjoyed the fine cool breeze of the harbor, the beautiful transparency of the waters allowing us to see shoals of fishes at a depth of fifteen feet— and the various styles of shipping, among which was a Spanish war steamer, with the broad pennant of a Vice Admiral, on a tour of inspection. At 2 p. m., came in sight the good steamer Rapido, which to-morrow makes us bid adieu to Trinidad. She comes but once a week from Havana, and a good opportunity occurs, with a pleasant party, of crossing the island, which we propose to embrace.

"why" such an unusual number of expeditions have lately been fitted out for the coast. The capture of three vessels filled with slaves, within something less than six weeks, has produced the greatest excitement in Havana, where some of the most influential of the dealers have ventured to demand *under what treaty and with what right* have American cruisers been permitted to take upon themselves the duties of a marine police in Spanish waters! The number of slaves lately captured and taken to Key West by the United States war steamers "Mohawk," "Crusader" and "Wyandotte," amount to about 1,800, averaging 600 for each vessel.

The salubrious air, mild and equable temperature and quiet of Trinidad, with refreshing music,
have done much to restore breath and vital forces
to our enfeebled body, and we shall ever remember it with gratitude to the All-wise Creator, who
has blessed us with returning health. We feel
strong enough to bear the journey, and the
change to the north side of the island, and to-
morrow we go to Cienfuegos, to take the railroad
for Sagua la Grande. Until we reach that port,
adios.

CHAPTER VIII.

"Oh! vale of bliss! Oh! softly swelling hills!
On which the power of cultivation lies,
And joys to see the wonders of his toil."

TRINIDAD DE CUBA, February 16, 1860.
The valley of the Trinidad Mountains extends
from this city about thirty miles, with a breadth
of four to six miles, and its rich and fertile
bosom is thickly dotted with the numerous settle-
ments of *ingenios* or sugar estates, owned by
wealthy planters, whose possessions are estimated
often by millions, and annual incomes by hundreds of thousands. We took the car of 6 a. m.,
and rode some 12 miles to *Manaca*, a noble
estate of Senor Isnaga, where we saw the whole
process of sugar making, from the crushing of
the cane to the packing of the sugar in hogsheads. The road passes, through many other
estates, where the negroes were cutting cane, and
hundreds of ox-carts hauling it to the mills. The
ride is through a most picturesque and lovely
6

valley, and the scenery varied and romantic. You pass through oceans of cane, with the grand palms scattered through the fields, looking like great sentinels guarding the rich possessions below them.

By special invitation, through the kindness of a friend, we started with him to make a visit to the estate of Don Miguel Cantero, about twelve miles off, in the valley. Three horses in our volante, under the guidance of an experienced *calesero*, whose short jacket and long sword gave him quite the appearance of preparation for business in cutting down any robbers who might attempt to stop his horses, formed our equipage. We were accompanied, also, by two horsemen; one from Philadelphia, the other from St. John's, N. B., who found that it required the constant aid of their spurs to keep their ponies up with ours, although with the heavy volante. We went at full tilt, jerking over rough roads and hills, as if we were endeavoring to escape pursuit, and in an hour and a half were received at the *quinta* by the senor with the affability and ease which characterizes the Cuban gentleman. Fortunately, he spoke our language fluently, and we were able the better to enjoy his hospitality, which was dispensed gracefully. A prime object of our visit was to see and examine a mineral spring on the estate, which we found on the bank of the charming river, mingling its sulphuretted stream with the limpid current of the latter—one identified with the sports of the people, which a new Governor, ignorant of their importance, has despotically invaded and set aside. The water of the spring is abundant, and strongly impregnated with sulphuretted hydrogen and carbonic acid, resembling much the water of the White Sulphur Spring, in Virginia. At some future day its medicinal virtues will make it a popular resort, and the beautiful estate on which it is will be an attractive and desirable place for invalids. Its occasional use in chronic skin diseases has caused its virtues to be appreciated in its immediate neighborhood, but it deserves a wider celebrity.*

At 10 a. m., after visiting the grounds, we enjoyed a most luxurious breakfast, combining American and Spanish cookery in its various dishes, whose profusion was enough for five times

---

* See note at the end of this chapter.

the number of our small party. Our agreeable
host then suggested a visit to a large estate or
ingenio, three leagues (or nine miles) off, and
ordered fresh horses. Our vehicle being properly
appointed, and our out-riders also accommodated, with the addition of our kind entertainer
on a rapid pacer, we started for the new desti-
nation. After coursing the hills and valleys, for
such was the speed, we arrived in an hour and
ten minutes, with no farther adventure than that
one of the horsemen, in crossing a river, got into
a hole, where his horse stuck fast, until he
jumped off, when the animal managed to get out.
He got off without further damage, except to his
suit of white linen, which suffered most extensively from the amount of mud necessarily dis-
turbed on the occasion.

The *ingenio* of *Guinea* is the property of
Senor Don Justo Cantero, a gentleman whose
name is identified with progress among a slow
and inert race of people, who are afraid of enterprise and exertion, as if they were principles of
destruction. Senor Cantero has imported from
France, at an expense of at least $100,000, the
machinery necessary for refining sugar, and has

introduced into this part of the island the only refinery here. We went through the various rooms, and saw the complicated and elaborate means of attaining the desired end, and followed the process through its details to the fine sugar in boxes, ready for export. Upon entering one of the rooms, we began to fix our tongue to muster up the little Spanish we possessed, to converse with a dark Spanish-looking, black-bearded individual, who seemed to have charge. Upon bowing to the senor, we were quite astonished at his "How are ye, doctor?" Upon enquiring how he had attained the knowledge of our dignified profession in that out-of-the-way region, he said, "I saw you in company with the officers of the Water Witch, going to Casilda, and heard them call you doctor, so I enquired about you; please to give my respects to Mr. R., when you return home to Columbia."

Let a Yankee alone for making discoveries wherever he is. Here was a New Bedford cooper, whó with his wife were residing on an *ingenio*, twenty miles from Trinidad, yet picking up quickly the knowledge of visitors to the latter place on an occasional visit. Our party called on

his lady, who was delighted to see folks that
could speak her language, having only her
parrot to do so in a limited way, during the
absence of her companion in his daily work.
She had resided here two years without leaving
the estate, and regretted our not staying the
night to have a long talk.

During the last week 3,600 pots of sugar
were turned out, and the yield of the season
is estimated at 5,000 boxes, worth $40 each,
or $200,000. Molasses and Muscovado sugar
made from it, pay the expenses of the estate.
On this estate are 340 negroes, of which number
about 200 go into the field. The amount of land
in sugar cultivation is about eight acres to the
hand, and the produce is as above stated. New
negroes are selling readily at $900 to $1,000
apiece, and the demand very great, which keeps
up the arrival constantly of cargoes, notwith-
standing the cruisers. When we visit the north
side of the island, we will describe the course of
proceedings on a sugar plantation more in
detail.

SULPHUR SPRING,

At the Quinta of Miguel Cantero, Trinidad Valley, Banks of the Ay.

Having no conveniences for the analysis of this water, we could only decide from our familiarity with the Springs of Virginia that the supply of sulphuretted hydrogen and carbonic acid was very large—of the former almost as much, and of the latter fully as much as in the water of White Sulphur Springs, Greenbriar County, Virginia. A bottle of the water was submitted to Messrs. Booth, Garrett & Reese, Analytical Chemists, Philadelphia, from whom the following letter was received:

PHILADELPHIA, June 29, 1860.

Dear Sir: We have made a careful qualitative analysis of the bottle of water which you left with us on the 22d inst.

The total solid matter per gallon is equal to 59.73 grains, and consists of muriates, carbonates and sulphates of lime and magnesia, with a small quantity of silex. We also examined closely for iodine, but were unable to prove its presence—

the water still retained a slight odor of sulphuretted hydrogen. The principal ingredient is *muriate of lime*, which constitutes perhaps one-third
of the whole solid matter. *Carbonate of lime*
was also present in large proportion, kept in
solution by free carbonic acid.

Yours respectfully,

BOOTH, GARRETT & REESE.

Dr. R. W. GIBBES, Columbia, S. C.

The Sulphur Spring alluded to, is situated on
the western bank of the Ay, at Sr. M. Cantero's
quinta, about 12 miles from Trinidad. The water
springs out from the side of the bank, and during
freshets is covered by the river's stream. It
could very easily be dammed, though most likely
other springs more favorably situated can be
found on the estate.

The presence of *muriate of lime* in much
larger proportion than in any of the Virginia
mineral springs, increases the value of this water
in scrofulous and glandular affections, as well as
in skin diseases and those of the liver, and we
believe it will be found highly therapeutic.

The spring is in a region of secondary blue limestone, resembling very much that in which most of the Virginia mineral waters are found. We see no reason why these waters should not come into use in the winter, as well as our own *White Sulphur* water in the summer, season.

CHAPTER IX.

" The traveler delighteth in the view
    Of change and choice of sundry kind of creatures,
  To mark the habits and to note the hue   ·
    Of far-born people, and their sundry natures,
  Their shapes, their speech, their gait, their features."

EN ROUTE TO SAGUA LA GRANDE,
February 18th, 1860.

THE COOLIES, &c.—In 1847, the Spanish Government issued an order allowing the importation
of 2,000 Chinese Coolies to supply labor in this
island, as an experiment; subsequently they allowed 2,000 more, and then removed any restriction as to number. The demand for labor is
great, and the increase of negroes on the plantations amounts to nothing, in consequence of
the great disproportion of the sexes, the women,
on many plantations, not amounting to one-fourth
of the number of slaves. The introduction of
Coolies has operated very injuriously in relation
to this increase, as none but males have been

brought, and, where they are employed on the plantations, their having money is a great source of corruption. The Coolies are sold by their importers at $350 to $400, and the purchaser buys them for eight years, paying to each in addition $4 per month.

There is a mart for Coolies at the CERRO, near Havana, which is open to visitors, but we did not visit it. They are used for all purposes. They are a sprightly, active and seemingly industrious people, very much in their intelligence and motions like our mulattoes. All can read and write. They make good mechanics, and are used as firemen on locomotives, brakesmen on cars, drivers of ox carts, water carriers, servants on board of the steamers, in Havana as waiters, and, also, as general laborers. As soon as they are out of their time they have the privileges of the whites, and you meet them riding in omnibuses, &c. They are docile, but many of them become discontented; and if so, or if whipped, they often commit suicide, having no regard for life.

One morning, when leaving Trinidad in the cars for a visit to the port Casilda, we saw several men carrying a coolie across the yard at the depot, and upon inquiry, found that he had taken poison. He ran away, a few days before, and on that morning was found in the car, near one of the stations, insensible. A tin cup was by him, containing something which he had taken; and the commissary of police brought it to the car, when we examined and found it *opium* and *aguadiente*, enough to kill half a dozen. The physician of the railroad was sent for to administer to him, but upon returning from Casilda, four hours after, we had the curiosity to go into the hospital, and found him dying. He died at 4 o'clock, and was taken to the cemetery at 6, two hours after! In the hospital were some twenty others sick with various complaints. They are much enervated by the climate, and being very slowly acclimatized, many die. The number who commit suicide is very large, and within a week we heard of two cases in Trinidad. The policy of the Government in allowing their introduction is a bad one, as in addition to the corrupting influence on the plantations, their intercourse with the lower class of Creoles will raise a population, with all the rights of the whites, that in the future will give trouble.*

The Spanish Government, while conniving at the slave trade, offers a premium for emancipation by its laws. Every negro owned is registered, and a price affixed for taxes; at this price, if the negro is dissatisfied, he can require his master to sell him, if he can find any one willing to buy him; or if he can save $50 to pay down, he can buy his freedom by installments, which the owner is obliged to receive. A mother can, by paying $50, buy an unborn child at any time, and the master is obliged to submit to it. Such cases occur in the towns and cities, but on the plantations the negroes are ignorant, and, without communicating with those who have a knowledge of the laws, they know little of them.

When a slaver is captured by a Spanish vessel, the negroes are called *emancipados*, and are sold, like the Coolies, for a term of years, and a great many become free in this way—the number of

---

* Since this was written the Captain General has issued an order of the Government, that the importation of Coolies shall cease at the close of this year.

free negroes on the island being very large, a
lazy, worthless set. You meet them in crowds at
every turn, and how they live is a mystery. The
emancipados are said to be not as well treated as
slaves, as their employers have no interest in
them beyond the term of service purchased.
The demand for labor on the plantations is very
great, and women being much wanted, sell for
the same price as men, and very readily. Lat-
terly, the importations have furnished more
females than formerly. The native born negro,
or Creole, is considered as far more valuable than
the imported African.

A recent correspondent of the N. Y. Herald
writes as follows:

"The local councils of the various districts are
about preparing reports in relation to the wants
of Cuba for additional labor, in order to keep
even with our vastly increasing product. Me-
morials, with ample specifications, illustrating
the condition of our general as well as agricultural interests, will be forwarded to the Government at Madrid, for the royal determination as to
the continued free introduction of voluntary emi-

grants from China, Indian Islands, Polynesian Islands (the straight haired negroes), or the coasts of Yucatan, under contracts for defined periods of service—eight years, more or less. The Coolie system, and this class of introduction, closes with the present year, according to the last royal edict upon the subject; and no remonstrance or excuse will be allowed for its continuance. However, as new 'bandas' are to be proposed for their government, more leniency in treatment, a slight advance in compensation, and social safety protected against redundant increase of the class— beyond the demand for labor and for security of the white population, having two antagonistic servile classes in their midst—it is possible that an extension may be granted for several years longer. We already begin to see idle and worthless Chinese in our streets in too large numbers for the safety of property. In Havana and suburbs, at this time, we have between 38,000 and 39,000 free negroes or colored; about 37,000 slaves, and 92,000 to 93,000 white persons—all told, nearly 169,000. The Chinese, occupied in the industry of the city, or residing here from termination or release from contract, are not as yet included in the census. The proportions, as they are, are not very pleasant to sleep upon; and the only safety we have, is the strong Government which keeps all colors and shades in order."

The arrival at our hotel of several men known to be engaged in the trade, induces the belief that a cargo is at hand, and will soon be landed. They are constantly arriving, and the facilities on a wide extent of coast are such that, with proper precautions, they can escape the war vessels. Over 40,000 were landed last year.

CHAPTER X.

"Fair nature! thee, in all thy varied charms,
Fain would I clasp forever in my arms!
Thine are the sweets that never, never sate!
Thine still remain through all the storms of fate!

CONCHA, THE PORT OF SAGUA LA GRANDE,
February 23, 1860.

No traveler has ever done, in one day, what our little party did yesterday—crossed the island of Cuba from the south to the north side. The railroad from Sagua to Las Cruces has been finished for some weeks, though a broken bridge has prevented the trains running over until now. We understood at Trinidad that on to-day the road connection with that to Cienfuegos would be celebrated, and the road opened to-morrow; so we proposed, instead of returning to Havana to go to Matanzas, to cross the island by the new road.

We left Trinidad at 8 a. m., in the fine steamer Rapido, and had a pleasant run near the shore to

7

the noble bay of Jagua, already noticed. The entrance is deep, but very narrow, covered by a strong and rusty-looking fort, of unplastered brick. We reached Cienfuegos at 1 p. m., and found a grand *dejeuner* going on during the cele- bration. Crowds had come over from Sagua, and the entertainment was a magnificent one, given by a citizen of Cienfuegos. A large hall was filled with fashionables, and the breakfast room adjoining had an immense table spread with luxuries, and ornamented with pyramids of arti- ficial flowers. The band in the area was pouring forth its melody, while the company was enjoy- ing the feast. We looked in upon the affair, and found an old friend present, and then proceeded to the hotel. Here we found the information of "no rooms," and upon inquiry learned that the festive party would return to Sagua at 3 p. m., and were politely invited to accompany it. Though the chances of lodging were as bad in Sagua, where there is no hotel, we determined that we could not be worse off, so we took the car.

The company was rather merry, and cham- pagne had put the senors into a somewhat bois-

terous humor, but we got through safely. The
road runs through a fine, hilly country, full of
sugar estates, but after visiting the valley of
Trinidad, the scenery was not very attractive.
We passed the great estate of *La Santa Susanna*,
which was said to have belonged to the Dowager
Queen of Spain before it was sold to the Havana
Company, which now owns it. They paid
$2,500,000 for it, and make annually 6,000
hogsheads of sugar. The machinery cost over
$200,000.

The train arrived at Sagua at 9 p. m., and here
it appeared that the Bishop of Havana had
arrived to consecrate the new Cathedral, and the
people were to have a three days' *fiesta*. Not a
cot was to be procured, and no accommodation
whatever could be found for our party of four.
The American Vice-Consul very politely offered
to give up his cot for one night, but that would
not have accommodated all, so we, fortunately
having a locomotive builder in our party, who
knew the engineer, he persuaded him to take us
in the tender to Concha, the port of Sagua, at the
mouth of the river, twelve miles off, where there
is a hotel. For the first time to three of the four

(one a lady), we rode upon trunks and logs of wood in the tender, over the roughest road we ever experienced, where the passenger cars daily run off the track—the engine, however, being heavy, rarely gets off. After severe jolting and jerking, and a threat of steam giving out, we reached the depot, within a mile of our hotel, about 12 p. m. Here we left trunks until morning, and, with carpet bags, took up our march over a *paseo*, or platform of boards, about four feet wide, upon piles, and after a reasonable time we got to the end of the bridge and our trials of the day—being the first party that ever made the trip from Trinidad across the island in one day.

Our hotel is built on piles, some distance out in the water, to be near the steamer's wharf, and presents the strangest looking settlement we have ever seen. The waters around are as clear as crystal, and we are surrounded by thousands of fishes swimming in every direction. In early morn, or after sun-down, the sardines are seen skipping in all directions. The bay is full of brigs and schooners, awaiting the arrival of hogsheads of sugar from the estates, and New

York and Philadelphia captains are abundant, and our only visitors. They bring out staves, hoop-poles and barrel heads, which are put together on the plantations or at the warehouses; and the estimate is, that it requires 30,000,000 of staves to supply this island alone.

Alongside of our house is a pen or *corral* of green turtle, which we suggested to our host was a welcome sight, having seen none on the south side. He said his Coolie did not understand cooking them. One of our party, Mr. N., of Philadelphia, undertook to instruct him, and after careful dissection of a fine fat fellow, he gave us the first dinner of turtle steaks and soup since landing on the island. Spanish cooking abounds in garlic, onions and highly-flavored Spanish oil, and saffron is largely used to color the soup and other dishes. Our three days detention at Concha has given our Chinaman cook instruction in broiling beef-steaks, frying fish and making turtle soup, and we trust future American visitors will be benefitted by his education, as these Coolies are very apt learners. This one has been five years in the country—long enough to get over the disposition to suicide. He turns up his nose at turtle, but he no doubt would smack his lips at a fat kitten or a plump rat. During the last two weeks, two Coolies in this place have hung themselves—one of them, because some one owing him five dollars went off without paying him. We find, wherever we go, that they are remarked for their vicious tendencies—drunkenness, smoking opium, stealing, &c.; a miserable population of a short-sighted Government.

As there was no attraction in Sagua, which is a poor place, we had no desire to attend the consecration of the Cathedral, to see the celebration by cock-fighting and playing *monte*. One of our party went up, and reported the state of things as very demoralizing. The *fiesta* lasts three days, and during this time cock-fighting, lotteries, raffles, and all sorts of street exhibitions, are going on. Some hundred tables were in the streets, at which senoras and senors were sporting the *onces* at *monte* or *loto*. At night, the Italian Opera was crowded to excess, and Miss Eliza Heron and her sister, from Philadelphia—calling themselves the Sisters Natalie—are the popular celebrities entertaining the citizens of Sagua.

The harbor of the port of Sagua (Concha) is

full of American barques and brigs, awaiting cargoes of sugar—the crop being very backward this year. With one of the Captains, we took a sail in his cutter to some of the *Cayos* or keys, in search of corals and shells; but found a poor beach and the mangrove so thick that landing was difficult, and we were not paid for our trouble by the few sponges and shells we found. On the way, we were amused at the huge unwieldy pelicans, flapping down into the water in all directions, tame enough to be shot with a pistol. Quantities of fine fish are taken in the seine by the sailors, among which the large *Pargo* and *Red Grouper* are conspicuous.

The arrival of the little steamer *Sagua*, on Wednesday, was the signal of our departure from the *boka*, and we bid adieu to Concha, Senor Lairo, our quiet, good-tempered and humorous host, and the sand-flies.

The desire to see somewhat of the interior of Cuba, induced our crossing the island, though with the prospect of difficulty and personal discomfort, instead of returning to Havana immediately. The *Sagua* is a small, flat-bottomed iron steamer, drawing about five feet water, and adapted to the perilous navigation among the keys, which are numerous on the coast. The first man who took a steamer through those *Cayos* must have been a fellow of infinite daring, as the narrow channels and short turns we experienced, were enough to deter another experiment of seeing the fine scenery, and having a sight of flamingoes and sea birds. Often our boat stuck for a time, and poles and backing, with occasionally a warp on the mangrove of the opposite side, were necessary to our extrication.

The water was beautifully transparent, and the bottom visible while among the keys. In many places the channel was scarcely twenty feet wide; however, we got through safely, with only an hour or two lost, instead of four or five days, as sometimes happens, and arrived at *Cardenas* to dinner. We have but little to say of this city, which is by no means conspicuous, except for mosquitoes and fleas. A very comfortable hotel is kept here by an English lady, but the place is low and hot, and presents no inducements for invalids to remain. There are sugar estates around, which are desirable residences.

We have mentioned the filthiness of the houses

of the Cubans—the steamer presented a shocking specimen of the kind. Senoras and horses, pigs and negroes, Spaniards and Coolies were huddled on board—in the ladies' cabin with them dirty negro women, with filthy children, were allowed the freedom of the berths—and in the gentlemen's cabin, twenty-four by twenty, were twenty-six berths, all occupied. The heat was excessive, tobacco smoke exuberant, and the jabbering of senors preventive of sleep. A fat priest, in a high humor, and a most disgusting commissary of night police from Matanzas, kept up such an incessant discussion to a very late hour, that no one could close his eyes, and when it ended, the latter commenced a snore on such a key that he must have practiced it before, to keep his deputies awake. The night was passed most disagreeably—the only one so since we landed on the island.

In the morning, after breakfast, the table was occupied as usual with *monte*, and gold was abundant. During the excitement of the game, a quarrel arose, which several attempted to quiet, but ineffectually—the disgusting snorer (a government official) was one of the parties, and getting very much excited, he slapped the face of the other, and was in turn slapped severely by a friend of the latter. The row seemed likely to become general, when the wife of one of them screamed and threw herself into the crowd, and the interference of gentlemen stopped the affair. It is expected that blood will be poured out as well as gold, and this is often the result of these gambling sprees in this vicious country.

The trip among the keys is very interesting once, and we appreciate it the more when safely over. The sea breeze is delightful, and the navigation smooth—the danger being of grounding in places where no assistance can be had.

We were all pleased to reach Cardenas, where we are now done with small steamers. Our next start is for Matanzas, and then for Havana by railroad, where the steamer for New Orleans will take us from a country, delightful for its climate to the Northern invalid, its beauty of scenery for the tourist, and its richness in production for its owners, but which stands sadly in need of a good government.

CHAPTER XI.

"O, ye bowers—
Ye valleys where the spring perpetual reigns,
And flowers unnumber'd o'er the purple plains
Exuberant showers—
How fancy revels in your lovelier domains!"

INGENIO—LA ARIADNE, NEAR MATANZAS,
February 27, 1860.

Cardenas was settled in 1827, and has grown up into a large city of ten thousand inhabitants. It has a fine bay, but is situated on low, flat ground, which makes it hot and remarkably productive of musquitoes. So far as wide streets are concerned, wide pavements and fine, handsome stores, it is the first city in Cuba, in our experience. The plaza is a fine one, the market the best we have seen, and the Cathedral in front of it quite imposing. The people have the reputation of more enterprise than in any other city on the island. A very good hotel is kept by Mrs. Woodbury, and you find English much spoken. The railroad to Bemba runs through a

beautiful country, filled with sugar estates, passing through immense fields of sugar cane, and
hundreds of acres of plantains, which are the
bread of the country, the main food of the
negroes,* though potatoes are also much de-
pended upon. Occasionally you see corn fields,
but the corn generally is not fine. Bemba is a
poor-looking place, scarcely worthy of being
called a town, but its neighborhood presents
beautiful scenery and rich *ingenios.* Here the
roads branch, one going to Havana, the other to
Matanzas—on the latter, the Coliseo Road, we
went to Matanzas, and found comfortable quarters at the Ensor House.

Matanzas is a fine city of 26,000 inhabitants,
and its magnificent bay gives it many advantages
to the numerous vessels always there. The old
and new towns are separated by the river *San
Juan,* spanned by solid and massive bridges, and
its banks are protected by masonry, giving it the
appearance of a wide canal. On a smaller scale,

---

* In a quaint old account of the land travels of D. Ingram in
1568, in the Gulf of Mexico, he says:

"There is a Tree called a Planten, wth. a fruite growinge on
yt like a puddinge, wch. is most excelent meate Rawe."

Matanzas somewhat resembles Naples, in its location on the bay. Matanzas being mainly settled by citizens from the United States, our language is more common there than in any other Cuban city, and the customs of the place are more Americanized. Many of the oldest residents are from the States. Fine equipages in New York style, with servants in livery with top boots, and fast trotters, in single and double buggies, sport in the *paseo* every evening. Volantes, however, of the handsomest kind, with their fantastic-looking *caleseros*, in laced jackets of all colors, and long boots highly ornamented with silver, are also popular. In the afternoon, when the troops are drilling, on the parade ground near the barracks, numbers of them, with three girls each, are flying around, enjoying the crowd and the music.

Matanzas is quite a handsome city, though, from its division by the river, it presents a somewhat disjointed appearance. The houses are many of three and even four stories, which are in contrast with those in the other cities of the island. We were particularly struck with the admirable counting houses of the merchants—so commodious, airy and cool. We have seen no where else such excellent rooms for business as the factors of Matanzas have.

As in all the others, the theatre is a prominent institution, and Rumsey, with his "Minstrels de Campbell," and Arthur Napoleon, with Mad. Vernay, a celebrated flutist, are vying with each other in entertaining the crowd. We find many visitors, attracted by the beautiful scenery of the Yumuri and the fine sea air. The latter is very agreeable when northers are not present, but they are frequent and make Matanzas not desirable for persons with pulmonary disorders. The temperature is often ten degrees below that of Trinidad, and 54° to 56° are not uncommon. The climate of Trinidad, free from northers and so equable, is far preferable. On arriving at Matanzas, we found a cool norther, and thick coats absolutely necessary—which we have not previously required. We dined with a most interesting family, and spent a pleasant day—upon leaving, we were kindly presented with a fine specimen of a *Chameleon*, which was caught in the dining-room. It breeds on trees in the gardens and woods, and is quite harmless.

Having letters to the hospitable proprietor of
La Ariadne, at Limcnar, we took the car at 9 a.
m., and arrived at his beautiful *ingenio* at 10½, in
time for breakfast, finding another party of visitors just returning from a morning ride—the
ladies in ecstasy with the easy pacing ponies.
We were received with great cordiality and a
hearty and courteous welcome, by Mr. A. C.,
the son, who manages the estate. After the full
descriptions, by Miss Bremer, Miss Murray and
Dana, of this admirably managed plantation, we
scarcely know what to say of it. We have
visited many and larger, but we have never seen
a sugar estate better ordered, or so systematically
administered. The arrangements are exact in all
departments, and carried out with ease and a
success which well repays the minute attention
of the manager. He is highly intelligent, well
educated in Paris, and by extensive travel,
and fully appreciating agricultural improvement
nothing is lost in the various processes, but
everything turned to account—the escape steam
is made to heat the reception pans of cane juice,
and if a horse dies, he is buried in the manure
pile, &c.

The process of sugar-making seems here to be very simple, and the machinery not at all complicated. The hands in the field, with a long knife, cut the cane close to the ground, top it, and throw it from them, to be taken up by others, who strip off the blades, and throw it into the ox-cart close by; when eight or ten carts are loaded, they go to the sugar-house, where the cane is emptied and piled around the press or crushing machine. This is fed by a wide trough, and as the cane passes through the press of three heavy cylinders, it is crushed and deprived of its juice, and falls into a cart below, to be hauled away and dried for fuel. It is then called *bagasse*, and is dried in piles, by the women, and covered with blades or housed—being the only fuel used for the furnace. It requires to be most carefully watched, as it is like tinder, and a fire is fatal to the hopes of the planter. The lower blades of the cane in the field being dry, ignite readily, and often the whole crop is swept by the work of an incendiary. Last year there were extensive fires, destroying many crops.*

---

* Recently an immense fire in the valley of Trinidad has destroyed cane to the value of a million of dollars.

It is said that, in some parts of the island, *black mail* is levied on the planters, and money freely given to buy exemption from villainous stipendiaries, known only by anonymous letters, demanding a tribute. Every precaution is necessary, in consequence of the danger of fire, and the police of the estates is essentially aided by numerous blood-hounds, which are turned loose at night to keep off strangers. They are very severe, and greatly feared.

The cane juice passes into reception pans heated by steam—now called *guarappa*—and then into other pans, called defecators, where lime is added to neutralize acidity. It then goes into a succession of boiling pans, and is skimmed—the scum passes into tanks, from which it is carried to the manure pile. The juice in the last pan, when of the proper proof, goes into large vats, and after standing twenty-four hours, cools into Muscovado sugar, and is put into hogsheads.

The hogsheads are carried into the draining or purging house, and having holes in the lower end, are placed on a floor of rack work, for the molasses to run into long troughs in a lower

8

story, terminating in tanks, from which it is put into hogsheads.

There are various estates on the island, on which clayed and refined sugars are made, and in preparing the latter, the machinery is very complicated. On Mr. C.'s estate, you have a fair specimen of a model establishment—though not large it is most efficiently worked. The visitor here has beautiful walks in the avenues of the Royal palm, of the ornamental mango, or the picturesque cocoa-nut or cocoa-palm. He finds in the variety of tropical fruits and flowers full occupation for his botanical knowledge, or he can study the huge black ant, so destructive, in its colonies and various characters of industrial pursuits. He can find the chameleon, the tarantula, the scorpion and the centipede of colossal proportions, to tax him farther—or in the woods and fields, birds which he has never seen before. The large oxen hauling immense wagons of cane heavily loaded, attract the attention, not only by the manner of being yoked by the horns, but by their admirable training. They are divided into two sections, one of which works a week, while the other rests, alternating with regularity.

They are of fine size and fat, and are the best specimens we have seen of the improved breed of the country. This estate is the only one we have visited where improved agriculture from older countries and book knowledge are adopted, and in all departments we see progress indicated.

The negroes are well looking and well cared for, which is not the case on some estates we visited. A large number of little ones is the evidence of good treatment, and a general healthiness seems characteristic of them. Our party was amused in seeing a crowd of children collected at the piazza, dropping upon their knees with the regularity of a drill by the old nurses, to receive the benediction of "old massa," who, in addition to the "*Adios*," usually gave each a biscuit, to their great satisfaction. We wish some of our Abolitionists at home could see these *blessings* in their proper light.

Returning from Limonar to Matanzas, we had the opportunity, next day, of visiting the *Cumbre*, a high ridge of mountains, from which the view is enjoyed of the romantic Yumuri Valley. Some of the party went in volantes and others on horseback, up the worst rocky road we

have ever seen—a disgrace to commissioners, if
such there be in this country, where most things
are totally neglected. As you ascend the Cumbre, the landscape below suddenly bursts upon
your view, with its sugar estates dotted over its
face, and the pea-green cane surrounding them,
contrasting most agreeably with the deeper
colored foliage of the tall palms and cocoa-palms,
scattered or in groups. The gentle undulations
of the valley—the streams meandering in the
distance, with the elevations of the *Pan of
Matanzas*, and its kindred hills, closing in the
rich area below, present a panorama of exquisite
beauty. We cannot compare it with the Valley
of Trinidad, so much more extensive; but more
circumscribed, it is not surpassed by any single
view in that luxurious region. For miles the eye
is filled with scenes of beauty, and the pictorial
creations of the pencil of the most imaginative
mind cannot present more novel artistic exhibitions of the gentleness and romance of nature's
scenery. A visit to the island is not complete
without enjoying the richness and magnificence
of the quiet beauty of the Valley of the Yumuri,
and a visit to a coffee plantation in the neighbor-

hood. The following description, by Ballou, gives a good idea of its interest:

"A coffee plantation is one of the most beautiful gardens that can well be conceived of; in its variety and beauty baffling correct description, being one of those peculiar characteristics of the low latitudes which must be seen to be understood. An estate devoted to this purpose usually covers some three hundred acres of land, planted in regular squares of eight acres, and intersected by broad alleys of palms, mangoes, oranges, and other ornamental and beautiful tropical trees.* Mingled with these are planted lemons, pomegranates, cape jessamines, and a species of wild heliotrope, fragrant as the morning. Conceive of this beautiful arrangement, and then of the whole when in flower; the coffee, with its milk-white blossoms, so abundant that it seems as though a pure white cloud of snow had fallen there and left the rest of the vegetation fresh and green. Interspersed in these fragrant alleys is the red of the Mexican rose, the flowering pome-

---

* The coffee-tree requires to be protected, at least partially, from the sun; hence the planting of banana and other trees in their midst.

granate, and the large, gaudy flower of the penon, shrouding its parent stem in a cloak of scarlet, with wavings here and there of the graceful yellow flag, and many bewitchingly-fragrant wild flowers, twining their tender stems about the base of these. In short, a coffee plantation is a perfect floral El Dorado, with every luxury (except ice) the heart could wish.

"The coffee-plant (*caffea Arabica*) is less extensively cultivated on the island than formerly, being found to yield only four per cent. on the capital invested. This plant was introduced by the French into Martinique in 1727, and made its appearance in Cuba in 1769. It requires some shade, and hence the plantations are, as already described, diversified by alternate rows of bananas, and other useful and ornamental tropical shrubs and trees. The decadence of this branch of agriculture was predicted for years before it took place, the fall of prices being foreseen; but the calculations of intelligent men were disregarded, simply because they interfered with their own estimate of profits. When the crash came, many coffee raisers entirely abandoned the culture, while the wiser among them introduced improved methods and economy into their business, and were well rewarded for their foresight and good judgment. The old method of culture was very careless and defective. The plants were grown very close together, and subjected to severe pruning, while the fruit, gathered by hand, yielded a mixture of ripe and unripe berries. In the countries where the coffee-plant originated, a very different method is pursued. The Arabs plant the trees much further apart, allow them to grow to a considerable height, and gather the crop by shaking the trees, a method which secures only the ripe berries. A coffee plantation managed in this way, and combined with the culture of vegetables and fruits on the same ground, would yield, it is said, a dividend of twelve per cent. on the capital employed; but the Cuban agriculturists have not yet learned to develop the resources of their favored island."

CHAPTER XII.

"Three hundred banner'd knights was indeed a gallant show;
Three hundred shaven Moors they killed, a man at every blow.
The Christians call upon St. James, the Moors upon Mahound;
There were thirteen hundred of them slain on a little plot of
ground."

HAVANA, March 3, 1860.

Steamers leave Matanzas every night for
Havana, and the cars every morning, occupying
about six hours in the transit. The road runs
through a country similar to what we have described from Cardenas—sugar cane and plantains
being the crops through which we passed. Occasionally, a small field of corn is visible. It is
yellow, but sweet, and makes passable hominy.

Arriving at Havana, we find the officials
"stirred up" grandly at news from Tetuan of a
great victory of the valiant Spaniards over that
small town. It takes very little to get up a
grand "funcion," and the bells are ringing, and
cannon firing from the Moro and the men-of-war
in the harbor, some of which seem to us sta-
tioned especially for such demonstrations. For

two nights, the palace of the Captain General has been brilliantly illuminated, as well as many houses in the neighborhood, and the Plaza thronged with crowds of fashionables and canaille, beggars in tatters, as well as crinoline, fine linen and broad-cloth. Four bands of music were out distributing melody, while the regular entertainment of the Plaza was dispensed as usual. In several of the streets, flags are extended across the whole extent, and Moors, hung by the neck, dangling in the air above you. These valiant people seem actually impressed with the idea that they have whipped all creation, and the proudest excitement pervades the masses.

For three days the *fiesta* is to be kept up, and as it is Lent, a dispensation has been granted, under the circumstances, by the Bishop of Havana, for a most elaborate and magnificent masked ball for to-morrow (Sunday!) evening, when the farce is to be closed until the next news. At the grand *"funcion taurica,"* bull- fight, on Sunday last, an incident occurred, which somewhat alarmed the three or four thousand spectators—a severe gust of wind came up, and the flag-staff was broken, and the Spanish flag, "blood and gold," actually fell into the arena—a bad omen—but the bull Tetuan, decorated by ribbons and ornaments from the hands of the *Condesa*, was killed, and the city is now reported as taken! What a coincidence!

A friend who happened to be at Matanzas gives us his experience there on the occasion of celebrating the victory:

"You Know Where, March 2d, 1860.
"*Dr. R. W. Gibbes.*

"Dear Sir: Since your departure we have had considerable excitement. The news of the fall of Tetuan has caused as much noise hereabouts as whilom that of Sebastopol. The Spaniards are doing their best to imitate the French in all things military. Read the court addresses, the army bulletins, the speech from the throne to the Cortes about the war, the subscription on foot for the army, and then take up similar documents from the other side of the Pyrenees, and with a few changes for dates and names, you have almost copies of the French addresses, speeches, &c. Thus it is with the great and glorious nation who, for the third time, (no doubt of it,) are saving the cause of civilization and christianity in Europe. A patriotic poet, after stringing together the largest amount of high-sounding and bombastic expressions the Spanish language can produce, recounting the glories of old, (!) (not having anything newer than Tetuan to speak of,) recalls the glorious achievements of the Cid against the Moors in days of yore, and winds off with a hint to the Yankees, most unmistakably pointed for their especial benefit. He says that some foolish nations have thought Spain dead, but beware! she has proved she was only sleeping, and has now arisen in her might to carry terror to the hearts of her foes! so I beg of you all to take your hats off and be civil, or else there is no knowing how soon your cities may not fall as fell Tetuan.

"By supreme decree, &c., &c., three days were set aside to celebrate the unparalleled achievement, and the bright spot which appeared on the escutcheon of Spain, so long doomed to mould and decay, was to be hailed as the harbinger of the resuscitation of the national honor. And so, for three days have all the guns, blunderbusses, pistols and cannon been roaring forth loud notes of praise to the heroic army who, in the face of unheard perils, trials under which other troops would have quailed, &c., &c., have so signally convinced the world (meaning themselves) that Spain has awakened to a new era of glory and power.

"In Matanzas, the proceedings were exceedingly noisy, and powder enough was expended in this one town to have blown the kingdom of Morocco, and Africa besides, over into the Pacific. The danger was imminent to those who had any business to attend to, as the glorious descendants of the Lions of Castile appeared perfectly reckless of the life and limbs of the passers-by, and most certainly appeared to me more like the asses of Castile clothed with the lion's skin. There were numerous balls, levees, dinners and other demonstrations to satisfy the eyes, the ears, the legs, and what appeared most difficult, the stomach, as those can testify who sat down to the entertainment at the Barracks, given by the officers of the garrison.

"A Moor in effigy was dragged about the streets, accompanied by a couple of policemen, and rag-tag and bob-tail bringing up the rear; at the street corners shots were fired at the fallen Moslem, with shouts for the army, the Queen, &c. One individual in the height of his patriotism, after several very effective discharges, thought to increase the noise and fun in proportion to the load of his arquebuss, and contrived to stop his own noise for some time, as the venerable piece of iron exploded, severely wounding him and scaring several others *into* their senses.

"As for the Cubans, I have seen none take any part in the demonstration; the balls in honor of the occasion were very poorly attended, and all appeared heartily glad when quiet once more resumed its sway. They certainly are aware that, no matter how the dance goes, they will have to pay for the music and the broken cups and saucers.

"What a bright idea it would be now, if the Government would just ship off to the scene of operations the several thousands of black troops now in such a beautiful state of discipline in the island, and try the valor of these worthy allies and comrades in arms of the defenders and heroes of Castile and Leon!

"I have some of the poetry written for the occasion, and should you desire, will forward translations." *

Havana is crowded with American visitors, mostly from our Northern States, avoiding cold weather, but they are embarking too early for New Orleans *en route* for home. The hotels are all full, and some difficulty is experienced in finding accommodations. The sailing of the *De Soto* for New Orleans, and a desire to avoid the risk of fancied equinoctial gales, two weeks hence, have caused somewhat of a stampede, and her state-rooms are all engaged.

CHAPTER XIII.

"So music past is obsolete—
And yet 'twas sweet! 'twas passing sweet!
But now 'tis gone away."

HAVANA, March, 1860.

In front of the Captain General's palace, which is a handsome and commodious residence, is the *Plaza de Armas* or public square, laid off handsomely and planted with beautiful trees, among which the royal palm is conspicuous, and rich flowers bloom. It is paved with flag stones and provided with benches, and in the evenings with chairs for the gay population to enjoy the music of the Government band. It is small but quite a handsome garden, and seems to be carefully attended. In the centre is a statue of "INDIA" surrounded by an iron railing, and across the street is a small chapel erected over the spot where Columbus is said to have first had mass on his landing. During the evenings, especially on

Sundays and feast-days, crowds congregate in the *Plaza* to promenade and hear the music.

Not far from the *Plaza* is one of the most important institutions of the city—the *Dominica*—one of the best ordered and most elegant *cafes* in the world. It is large enough to accommodate in its marble hall several hundred persons at one time, and is the resort of almost every body at some time of the day. In the centre is a fountain; and in all directions you find marble tables of various sizes and shapes to accommodate parties suitably. Call for "chocolate," or "cafe," or "*dulces*," or ices, or the delicious orange *granizada*, or the lemon *panalis*, or cakes of endless variety, and you are served with the accompaniment of the puff of a rich *Habana* or a delicate *cigarillo* from the next table. Every body smokes except yourself, perhaps, and the presence of ladies is "*nada*"—they smoke, too, if they please. Surrounded by representatives of all nations and peoples and tongues, you have a jargonic noise, in which the loud voice of *Los Espanoles*, with their rich, sonorous intonation, largely predominates. The *Dominica* is the meeting-place of friends at any hour, and you see the crowd at that very time.

Having enjoyed the luxuries of this grand cafe, you step across the street to see the manufactory of *dulces*, and before you enter you are regaled with the rich atmosphere of *guava* that pervades the neighborhood. Here you find steam engines at work to supply the world with jellies and marmalades, and preserves of all the fine fruits of the island. The foreign business is immense, and the quantities of huge boxes constantly handed out to the wagons at the doors attest the fact.

Next to the essential *Dominica*, the most attractive resort of the Cuban, is the "*Teatro de Tacon*," a splendid and spacious building a short distance beyond the walls, opposite *El Campo Militar*, adjoining the Paseo Isabel—leading to the longer called *Paseo Tacon*, a mile long, so called from its projector. The external appearance of this theatre is not striking, but the tasteful arrangements within are particularly so. The light iron columns and railings, and open formation of the boxes, give an airiness to the building especially adapted to a warm climate,

9

and the accommodation of three tiers of boxes and two galleries is extensive—the pit alone having separately numbered seats for one thousand persons. It is well constructed for speaking, and the exhibitions are very effective. The decorations are costly, and the frescoes and side ornaments of the proscenium beautiful. From "grave to gay"—or rather, from the gay to the grave—we pass through the outer gate, *Puerta del Punta*, to the *Campo Santo* or public burying-ground, where rich and poor have their bones alike placed, though not in their last resting-place. The former are shoved into niches or oven-like recesses in the thick inner wall, and the latter are placed coffinless in the ground in shallow graves, and are sprinkled with lime to hasten decomposition, so that their bones may easily be removed to make room for others. Respect for the dead is not characteristic of Cubans, and this may be seen exemplified on any afternoon by any visitor to the *Campo Santo* of Havana.

Next to the prison-house of the grave is one of Tacon's public works, which characterised his administration—the *Presidio* or prison, erected of yellow stone outside the walls, near the fortress of the *Punta*. It is built in the form of a parallelogram two hundred and forty feet front by three hundred feet deep—and on the eastern front on the left contains the dwelling-house of the Alcalde, and on the right the *Cuerpo de Guardia* or guard room. Arrangements exist to separate the whites and colored prisoners, and those who can pay get somewhat different accommodation from others, though there appeared no provision for sleeping but on the stone floor.

The *Paseo de Tacon* alluded to above extends to the CERRO, formerly a village on a height, about three miles from the city, but it is now a part of the suburbs—the *barrios estra muros* exceeding the city within the walls, and having wider streets.

The *Baños Publicos*, in this warm climate and dusty city of Havana, are worthy of special notice. On the way to the *Campo Santo* you pass several in the *Calzado san Lazaro*. They are cut out of the solid limestone rock, on the edge of the coast, in spaces of about twenty feet square and three to eight feet deep, the outer wall perforated with holes to allow the water to flow in and out. The temperature of the water of the Gulf stream which supplies them is about 72°, and the danger of sharks makes this provision for bathing essential to safety. There are separate baths for females, and for persons of color—all which are covered by a wooden roof. There are, also, bath houses in Havana, where you have warm or cold baths for the moderate charge of 25 cents—one near Le Grand's Hotel, where the entrance is through a billiard room, is much patronized by Americans, both ladies and gentlemen.

Of the institutions of learning in Havana, the chief is "The University," founded in 1728 and re-organized in 1842. It is intended chiefly for law and medical students; has some thirty professors, and the foundation of a cabinet of natural history—insects, minerals, fossils, shells, &c. It possesses a small library containing some valuable books, which is quite respectable for its size. The building is a very commodious one, in the form of a hollow square, with a garden containing many interesting plants.

Access can be had to it at any time without a

permit, but a letter to one of the professors is always desirable.

There are several Institutes or Colleges for the branches of secondary education, as well as primary schools. One of the principal literary establishments is the Seminary of St. Charles, founded in 1774, where a limited number of young men are educated for the ecclesiastical profession. The instruction is confined to Latin, Natural Philosophy and Theology.

Much improvement in public education has taken place since the establishment of the Economical Societies of Havana and Santiago de Cuba. The object and purposes of these societies were "to promote agriculture and commerce, the breeding of cattle, the industry of the country in general, and, as occasion offered, the education and instruction of youth."

These institutions have, however, not been as successful as they should have been, in consequence of jealousy on the part of the Government. They have, however, founded and led to several important charities—the *Casa de Beneficenza*, or Charity Home—the *Casa Cuna*, or

Foundling Hospital—and the *Casa de Locos,* Insane Asylum.

In Havana there are five daily papers, and one weekly. In Matanzas there are two daily papers—in Trinidad one, the *Correo.* In San Espiritu is a daily paper, and in other towns, commercial reports, economical sheets, are occasionally published.

With a party of ladies and gentlemen, we visited the fortresses of the *Moro* and the *Cabanos,* and received the politest attention from the colonel commandant of the latter, who accompanied us and explained the several departments. The *Moro* is a strong fort, on the top of a limestone rock, and commands the entrance to the bay. It was first built in 1633, but was destroyed by the British, in 1762. The present structure was then rebuilt. On it is a lighthouse, and within its walls are dungeons for prisoners condemned for grave offences. The *Cabanos* is the great fortification opposite to Havana, extending around the bay for nearly half a mile. It was forty years a-building, and is chiefly hewn out of the solid blue limestone, and is immensely strong. The barracks are on each side of the extensive *paseo*, and the cells for prisoners, many of whom are sent here; the commandant said there were not less than a thousand at present. There are accommodations for 10,000 troops, and as many more can be provided for in tents, as the area within the walls is very extensive. The water cisterns under it extend a long distance, and are capable of supplying a long siege. The number of guns mounted is very large, and they are heavy— among them are large guns bearing the names of the twelve apostles. The depots of balls covered up by mason work, are numerous, and the quantity must be very large; the magazines of powder are also extensive. The officer, in showing us around, led us through a perfect town in extent, and politely took us to the finest positions on the bastions to enjoy the scenery. The view of Havana is, as he termed it, "*immenso grande,*" and presents a picture of rare beauty. We are not surprised at the pride of the Spaniards in their beautiful island, which, in air and scenery, cannot well be surpassed; and in fortresses is abundantly supplied. The cost of those above mentioned is said hyperbolically to have been $160,000,000—nearly as much as has been proposed to be given by our Government for the whole island. We ought to own Cuba, which would richly repay its cost at double that sum. A liberal government is greatly wanted, and Spain would be relieved of a heavy burden by its sale, while we could treble its productions in a few years, and make the whole island a perfect garden. The pertinacity of President Buchanan, in keeping its purchase before Congress, is probably based on the fact that there is a growing party in Spain, in favor of selling it; and ere long the proposition may not be offensive to the proud Castilians.

"Regla," which is located on the other side of the harbor, opposite to Havana, formerly was notorious as the resort of a gang of pirates, whose atrocities on the coasts of this island became so flagrant, that the Governments of the United States and England determined to send a combined squadron to root them out, which they did most effectually. The last case of piracy occurred off Cape "San Antonio," in the year 1839, when a Halifax brig, bound from Jamaica to Nova Scotia, fell into their power; all hands were murdered, except one man, who swam to the shore and gave information which led to the capture of the pirates, all of whom were executed at Havana. Regla can now boast of splendid stores for the deposit of sugar; fine, substantial wharves, and many other shipping facilities, which will, in the course of a few years, make it a very formidable rival to Havana.

CHAPTER XIV.

"When first his drooping sails Columbus furled,
And sweetly rested in another world."

We visited frequently the noble old cathedral of San Ignacio, and admired its stately arches and fine frescoes. Mass is performed every morning at eight o'clock, which is a favorable time for a visit. After this service, the old building—200 years old—can be inspected, and its fine pictures seen, of which there are several of great merit. Among them is a good painting of *San Christobal*, the patriot saint of Havana, bearing on his shoulder the infant Jesus with the world in his hand. Another is of *Maria Conceptionis*, the patroness saint of the cathedral, standing on the world and crushing the serpent's head with her heel. The finest work, however, is a *Virgin and child* offering an olive branch to several persons in purgatory. It is well painted and very expressive. The floor is

of variegated marble, and the high altar a pil-
lared dome of rich Egyptian porphyry.

The old *sacristan* who shows you around,
presents you with a card—*una papelita de
Colon*—on which you have a copy of the slab
over the remains of the great Christobal Colon—
with a memorandum of his life, and various in-
terments; for this, he expects a present of a
peseta from you in return.

In the rear of the cathedral is a college for
boys, where there are about forty in training for
the priesthood. In the quadangular area is quite
a pretty garden. The cathedral is a fitting mau-
soleum of Christobal Colon, whose ashes, in an
urn, are enclosed in a niche within its walls.
The spot is on the right side of the great altar,
and is marked by a basso relievo, in white
marble, of the great commander, with the following inscription:

O Restos e Ymagen del gran Colon!
Mil siglos durad guardados en la Urna
Y en la remembranza de nuestra Nacion.

Upon leaving the cathedral, one morning, we
thought of taking home a memorial in the form
of a bronze statuette, or an engraved portrait of

the great admiral, but we searched the stores of
the city ineffectually, nothing of the kind being
known in Havana! We recollect a few years
since hearing from a friend who had resided at
Genoa, that there was no authentic bust or portrait of the great Columbus in his native city!
It is a poor excuse that he left it in early youth,
and became distinguished after the age of fifty.

As everything relating to this remarkable man
deserves to be well known, we have concluded to
give the following account of the ceremonies on
the occasion of the reception of his remains at
Havana. Dr. Wurdeman says:

"The Spanish account, published at the time
in Havana, and which is now out of print and
very rare, describes the ceremonies attendant on
their reception as having been conducted with
much pomp. On the arrival of the vessel, the
whole population of the city came forth to receive them; and the ecclesiastical, civil, and
military bodies vied with each other in rendering
honor to them. On the morning of the 19th of
January, at nine o'clock, three lines of barges
and boats from the vessels of war, dressed with

mourning, were seen approaching the Mole. One, occupying the centre, bore a coffin, covered with black velvet, ornamented with fringes and flakes of gold, and guarded by a company of marines. It was brought on shore by the captains of the vessels, and received by the city authorities. Alternately borne by four of the most distinguished citizens, it was conveyed to the Plaza des Armas, in front of the column erected there by the city, in commemoration of the first mass which, according to tradition, had been celebrated on that spot.* It was here placed in an ebony sarcophagus, having the form of a throne, beautifully wrought with gilt carvings. This was supported by a bier twelve feet long and five high, covered with folds of black velvet, ornamented with golden flakes and lacings; while from the four corners of the sarcophagus as many golden cords hung, terminating in tassels of the same material, which were held by those, who, in their turn, had the

---

* The tree under which many of the good Habaneros believed that Columbus said mass, is now removed; and a chapel is erected ou the spot, in commemoration of the same; in front of this stands the column.

honor to escort the remains. Around this, six long, thick wax candles continually burned; they were supported on cornucopias, of the same wood and workmanship as the sarcophagus. The pavements were carpeted around this sombre spectacle, and beside it was a table covered with black velvet, supporting three cushions of the same material fringed with gold, and thirty-six lighted wax tapers.

"The coffin having been placed on this, the Governor, the Captain General, and the commander of the royal marines approached, and by order of the first it was opened. Within was seen a gilt leaden chest, about a foot and a half square, and one high, secured by an iron lock. This was opened by a key, and disclosed a plate of the same metal, and a small piece of bone, which, with the ashes it also contained, was evidently that of a body. These were then formally pronounced by the Governor, and the other illustrious examiners, to be the remains of the *incomparable Almirante Christoval Colon.* It was now closed and locked, and put into its coffin; and the latter having been replaced in the ebony sarcophagus, the procession was formed and proceeded towards the cathedral, from which the music and responses were occasionally heard borne on the passing breeze.

"In front were four field-pieces, drawn by eight pair of black mules arrayed in mourning, and led, each by one footman. These were followed by four white horses, caparisoned with fine black cloth bordered with gold, and decorated with the escutcheon and arms of Columbus, each likewise led by two footmen. Behind rode the Colonel and Lieutenant-Colonel, sword in hand, at the head of the grenadiers and militia. Then came the cross of the cathedral, escorted by seven orders of monks, the clergy, and the venerable ecclesiastical chapter; the bier, carried by eight men, and followed by the Captain General and other civil officers; the guard of honor, the military staff, and the citizens; the whole surrounded by a body of dragoons. The streets through which they passed were decorated with suitable emblems, and the walls of the houses hung with drapery; while salvos of artillery and volleys of musketry were continually fired by the armed vessels and garrison, until the termination of the whole ceremony.

"Conducted with this pomp, the coffin was conveyed to the cathedral, the pall-bearers holding the golden cords of the sarcophagus, being frequently relieved by others; for the proud of the land eagerly sought, if but for a short time, the honor of this office. The whole church was carpeted; numerous large wax candles placed at regular distances, by their lurid light, added to the sombre air it presented; while the altar literally blazed with the flames that burned on and around it. The massive columns and the doors were covered with banners with expressive designs and verses inscribed on them, relating to the history and death of the great discoverer of America; and in the centre of the church, under the dome, a pantheon forty feet high and fourteen long, erected for the temporary reception of the remains, by the splendor of its decorations, added not a little to the grandeur of the whole. The coffin having been deposited on a stand, amid twenty large wax tapers, at the door of the cathedral, was there received by the diocesan, Don Felipe Joseph de Trespalacios, dressed in an ample black cloak, and was conveyed to the pantheon amid the solemn music of the church,

the responses of the chapter, and the masses,
which from day-break had been said for the
repose of the soul of the dead.

"We have already adverted to the beauty of
the pantheon. It was of the Ionic order; the
lower part resting on a socle three feet high; was
composed of sixteen columns in pairs, four on
each side; the pedestals and capitals harmoniz-
ing with the friezed architecture and cornice.
The columns, imitating white marble, were gilt
and bronzed above; and over the cornice on
each side was a frontispiece, with passages in
the life of Columbus figured in bass-relievo.
Above this, on a pedestal, with a vignette of a
crown of laurels and two olive branches, an
obelisk was erected. At its foot, the escutcheon
and arms of Columbus were figured, while it was
further ornamented by three figures:—Time with
his scythe and hour-glass, but having his hand
tied behind him,—Death, the conqueror of all,
himself prostrate,—and Fame, her right hand
holding a serpent, in the shape of a circle, the
emblem of eternity, and her left, a clarion, with
which she proclaimed the glory of her hero,
immortal in defiance of Time and Death. The

10

arches also contained figures,—a weeping Genius in front, and on the sides, nautical trophies.

"On the sides of the obelisk not occupied by the figures, medallions, imitating grey jasper, were inlaid, having the following inscriptions:

"'Christophori de Colon cineribus ex Dominicano Insula, quam ditioni Castellæ detexit ac subjugavit huc translatis in perpetuæ gratitudinis signum Havana civitas hoc monumentum erexit, A. D. MDCCXCVI.'

"'Siste viator magni Christophori Colombi ex Insula Sancti Dominici translatæ hic cineres iacent. Mirabile Visu!'

"'Havana civitas in pignus gratitudinis æternæ hoc monumentum extulit in translatione cinerum Christophori de Colon, ex Dominicani Insula, Anno Domini, 1796.'

"On each side of the socle, a stair of four steps, in imitation of grey jasper, led into the interior of the pantheon, where the sarcophagus, already described, was placed; while between the columns, folds and loops of black velvet, fringed with gold, hung in festoons. On the sides of the bier were placed two statues, resembling white marble, and larger than natural. One represented Spain as a beautiful matron, with the imperial crown, and dressed in a flow-ing robe, embroidered with castles and lions; her right hand grasping two sceptres, and her left pointing to two worlds. The other, America, with her bow and quiver, and her plumed crown; evincing by her posture, the gratification with which she acknowledged the dominion of Spain. At the head of the bier, a gilt tablet contained the following epitaph :

"'D. O. M. Claris. Heros. Ligustin. Christophorus Columbus a se, rei nautic. scient. insign. nov. orb. detect. atque Castell. et Legion. regib. subject. Vallisol. occul. xii. kal jun. A. M. DVI. Cartusianor. Hispal. cadav. custod. tradit. transfer. nam ipse prescrips. in Hisponiolœ Mœtrop. ecc. hinc pace sancit. Galliœ reipub. cess. in hanc V. mav. concept. imm. cath. ossa trans. maxim. om. frequent. sepult. mand. xiv. Feb. A. MD. C. CX. CVI. Havan. Civit. Tant. vir. meritor. in se non immem. pretios. exuv. in optat. diem tuitur. hocce monum. erex Presul. JLL. D. D. Phillippo JPH. Trespalacios civic. ac militar. rei gen. præf. exmo. D. D. Ludovico de las Casas.'

"All the cornices of the frontispiece were illuminated, as well as the angles of the obelisk, to its summit; while below, surrounding the whole pantheon, a hundred large wax candles on stands

of a suitable size, and above, as many more, cast
their lights on the golden ornaments.   The union
of the whole, and the exquisite appearance of
each particular part, presented to the eye a mass
of sombre magnificence, that elicited the admiration of all the spectators.   The service of the
dead was now solemnly chanted, and mass celebrated by the pontifical and illustrious diocesan,
which was followed by the funeral oration, delivered by Don Joseph Augustin.   The last
responses were then chanted, accompanied by
solemn music; and the coffin, borne by the Field
Marshal, the Intendente, and other high officers,
was conveyed to its destined resting-place in the
walls of the church, as already described, and
the opening to the cavity closed by the marble
slab.

"Thus terminated the ceremonies of the day;
more remarkable for their object, than for the
extraordinary concourse of people, of both sexes,
who filled the streets, the Plaza, and the Church;
and the universal homage which the high and
the low alike paid to the memory of departed
worth.   The resting-place of him whom five

cities claimed as a son, is, moreover, by this record clearly marked; and a picture of the earlier days of Havana, although only a partial one, presented to us. It is also remarkable that, amid all the designs inscribed on the banners, but one contained a slight allusion to the persecutions which this brave man suffered from his sovereigns; as if silence could efface the stain they left on the escutcheon of his country. One of the banners bore a palm-tree loaded with chains, and the motto, 'Adversus pondera surgo.' A note to this states that '*El creer muchos que el Almirante murio preso y que fue enterrado con los grillos, nace de que jamas los perdio de vista, pues siempre los conserve en su retrete; y asi miamo, pidio por clausula en su testamento, que los enterrasen con ellos.*' No mention is made of any fetters having been found with his remains in the cathedral of St. Domingo, and his ashes were transferred to the silver urn, that now holds them, on the adoption of the new constitution by Spain. At the same time a copy of it was placed in the leaden chest, and the old stone removed for the one that now closes the opening in the wall, and which bears the following inscription:

"O restos é imágen del gran Colon!
Mil siglos durad guardados en la Urna
Y en la remembranza de nuestra nacion."*

The most authentic portrait of Colon in the United States is a copy of that in possession of the Duke de Veráguas, the descendant and present representative of the family, which was brought from Spain by the Hon. Mr. Middleton, formerly Minister. A fine copy, by Chapman, is in the possession of Gouverneur Kemble, Esq., at Cold Spring, near West Point, N. Y. It represents him as of fair complexion and light hair, while the ordinarily received portraits present him as of dark skin and swarthy.

It is a singular coincidence that the remains of the two greatest men, made illustrious by the discovery of America, should have been removed

---

* What, after all, if these are not the ashes of Columbus! There was neither inscription nor sign on the leaden chest or plate, by which the enclosed remains could be certainly identified,—the account mentions none; this, however, were heresy in Havana.

and reinterred about the same time during the close of the eighteenth century. The following from Mr. Prescott's Mexico, as to the removal of Hernan Cortes, is a suitable accompaniment to the foregoing:

"THE INTERMENT OF THE MARQUESS OF THE VALLEY OF OAJACA, HERNAN CORTÉS, AND OF HIS DESCENDANT, DON PEDRO CORTÉS, WHICH TOOK PLACE IN THIS CITY OF MEXICO, FEB. 24, 1629.

"The remains of Don Hernan Cortés, (the first Marquess of the Valley of Oajaca,) which lay in the monastery of St. Francis for more than fifty years since they had been brought from Castilleja de la Cuesta, were carried in funeral procession. It also happened, that Don Pedro Cortés, Marquess of the Valley, died at the court of Mexico, Jan. 30, 1629. The Lord Archbishop of Mexico, D. Francisco Manso de Zuñiga, and his Excellency the Viceroy, Marquess of Serralbo, agreed that the two funerals should be conducted together, paying the greatest honor to the ashes of Hernando Cortés. The place of interment was the church of St. Francis in Mexico. The procession set forth from the palace of the Mar-

quess of the Valley. In the advance were
carried the banners of the various associations;
then followed the different orders of the religious
fraternities, all the tribunals of Mexico, and the
members of the Audience. Next came the
Archbishop and the Chapter of the cathedral.
Then was borne along the corpse of the Marquess
Don Pedro Cortés in an open coffin, succeeded
by the remains of Don Hernando Cortés, in a
coffin covered with black velvet. A banner of
pure white, with a crucifix, an image of the
Virgin and of St. John the Evangelist, embroidered in gold, was carried on one side. On
the other were the armorial bearings of the King
of Spain, also worked in gold. This standard was
on the right hand of the body. On the left hand
was carried another banner, of black velvet,
with the arms of the Marquess of the Valley
embroidered upon it in gold. The standard-
bearers were armed. Next came the teachers
of divinity, the mourners, and a horse with sable
trappings, the whole procession being conducted
with the greatest order. The members of the
University followed. Behind them came the
Viceroy with a large escort of cavaliers; then

four armed captains with their plumes, and with pikes on their shoulders. These were succeeded by four companies of soldiers with their arquebuses, and some with lances. Behind them banners were trailed upon the ground, and muffled drums were struck at intervals. The coffin enclosing the remains of the Conqueror was borne by the Royal Judges, while the knights of the order of Santiago supported the body of the Marquess Don Pedro Cortés. The crowd was immense, and there were six stations where the coffins were exposed to view, and at each of these the responses were chanted by the members of the religious fraternities.

"The bones of H. Cortés were secretly removed from the church of St. Francis, with the permission of his Excellency the Archbishop, on the 2d of July, 1794, at 8 o'clock in the evening, in the carriage of the Governor, the Marques de Sierra Nevada, and were placed in a vault, made for this purpose, in the church of Jesus of Nazareth. The bones were deposited in a wooden coffin inclosed in one of lead, being the same in which they came from Castilleja de la Cuesta, near Seville. This was placed in another of crystal, with its crossbars and plates of silver; and the remains were shrouded in a winding-sheet of cambric, embroidered with gold, with a fringe of black lace four inches deep."

At high mass, after the news of the victory at Tetuan, we were present, but were disappointed at the music, the organ not being worthy of so fine a cathedral.

Apropos des bottes, speaking of music, our last evening in Havana was at the great *Tacon Theatre*, where we enjoyed the fine music of *Los Puritanos*. Gassier was prima donna; but her voice was not equal to the music. The theatre is beautiful and admirably arranged, as before mentioned, but its size is below that of the Academy, in New York, though it is said to hold 10,000 persons. This, however, is the exuberance of Spanish fancy.

Upon leaving Havana, we were desirous of selecting a few fine cigars to distribute among friends, and upon enquiry, we found the finest were $300, and the next quality $255 per thousand! Zounds, what a price! We contented ourself with those at $50, and almost wished we could appreciate Odoherty in *Noctes Ambro-sianæ*, where he says:

> "Sublime tobacco, which, from east to west,
>   Cheers the tar's labors, or the Turkman's rest;
>   Which on the Moslem's ottoman divides
>   His hours, and rivals opium and his brides;
>   Magnificent in Stamboul, but less grand,
>   Though not less loved in Wapping or the Strand.
>
> "Divine in hookahs, glorious in a pipe,
>   When tipped with amber, mellow, rich and ripe,
>   Like other chârmers wooing the caress
>   More dazzlingly when daring in full dress;
>   Yet thy true lovers more admire by far
>   Thy naked beauties—Give me a Cigar!"

He may have said *Buy* me one. As a matter of courtesy the Government officials allow 500 for personal use to pass free of duty. If you have more you are charged.

CHAPTER XV.

"How small the choice from cradle to the grave
  Between the lot of hireling help, or slave!
  To each alike applies the stern decree
  That man shall labor whether bond or free.

  The negro freeman, thrifty while a slave,
  Loosed from restraint becomes a drone or knave,
  Each effort to improve his nature foils,
  Begs, steals, or sleeps and starves, but never toils."

In reply to questions as to free labor and the Coolie system, a friend, an intelligent Cuban, writes as follows. The letter is interesting, and worth including among our notes:

"We are very poorly off as regards white help here, from causes I narrate below. In days by-gone, the place of overseer, or mayoral, as it is called here, was in the hands of creoles of the island, born mostly on estates under management of their fathers, and thus the accumulating experience of each being handed down from father to son, rendered them fully competent to under-

stand the proper system of managing large gangs
of negroes, and also to carry on all the works of
an estate. But since a few years, this class has
been disappearing gradually from this part of the
country, going towards the eastern end, and now
this delicate and important situation is thrown
into the hands of natives of Old Spain, or of
Islenos, (Canary Islanders,) generally having
been sent out here by ship-loads to serve out
their time by contract—a most debased and de-
moralized class, lower, intellectually, than the
creole-negroes they are to govern, and to whom
lying and deceit are as life and breath. Men
born with one *solitary idea*, and as incapable of
conceiving a *new one* as of squaring the circle.
At this we cannot wonder, for what can be expected of the dregs of a nation where the best
are but noted for profound ignorance, bigotry
and moral decay?

"One can easily imagine the consequences of
such example in the governed class, and the state
of affairs is most trying and wearing to any one
who wishes to "get along," and at the same time
is in a measure obliged to have recourse to such
elements. Add to this, that no one, unless in

actual want, will turn a hand to useful and continued employment, where the cock-pit or gambling table can afford excitement and food, and
one must feel surprise at the immense number of
idlers, whose only occupation consists in dealing
cards or matching cocks.

"Another most disastrous act in its future
bearing upon the destiny of Cuba, is the importation (now suppressed) of Chinese laborers, a
most worthless set, as far as labor goes, and a
most dangerous one to our heterogeneous society,
when their total disregard of life to themselves
or to others, and the absence of every moral or
religious restraint is taken into consideration, as
proves the immense increase of crime in every
shape, and of which the greatest amount is of
their committing. They are always found, after
serving their time out, in little communities on
the outskirts of towns, forming associations of the
most dangerous character against the safety and
order of the community they inflict with their
presence; and a most serviceable piece of business on the part of Government would be the
transportation of such as are out of employment
back to the Celestial Kingdom. Estimates care-

fully made on neighboring estates (ten) give an incredible item of mortality among them, viz: Among 470 Coolies imported on these places, the loss amounted to 48 per cent., of which 19 per cent. were from death by suicide, 7 per cent. from effects of use of opium, 4 per cent. run away or not accounted for, and the remaining 18 per cent. from death by disease; and I am told by credible persons that the mortality is still greater on the large places in the interior.

"We have, at last, the first of *numerous reforms promised* by the Home Government, but which I believe are like the cakes or sweets promised to quiet a crying child. I allude to the first public trial of a criminal case in Cuba. Formerly, prisoners were placed in jail, and witnesses also, without regard to even the most important business, without even being allowed to see a friend, or communicate with one, and there left to await the slow progress of Spanish law, often leaving the cell for the tomb, from diseases contracted in the unwholesome cell. Where judges, not accountable to any one for their proceedings, received large bribes to favor one or the other party, to the exclusion of all justice, the utmost corruption of law must exist; but where, in a measure a sort of publicity is given to their decision by an open trial, they cannot flagrantly violate existing laws at their pleasure, and without incurring a degree of censure which no one will risk doing openly.

"These changes are most essential in Cuba, to preserve the peace of the island, as intelligence and civilization are sworn enemies to the old despotic rules. Bigotry and prejudice can erect no barrier that can resist the advance of reform political, and only do we find that obstinacy against improvement in the degenerate old Catholic monarchies, which time will eventually sweep away, to make room for more equitable and generous systems of government. The great tidal wave of knowledge is resistless in its course.

"In intelligence and education, the Creoles are far ahead of their forefathers of the land of garlic and castanets; and as the ideas imbued in foreign education and travel get disseminated and take root amongst the lower class, a new order of things must inevitably take place. It is for the mother country to foresee and forestall all desired innovations, and Cuba will remain

Spanish; otherwise the Spanish crown will lose its brightest jewel.

"Lopez failed, it is true, but his very failure, and the *eclat* given to his act, by the undisguised alarm of the Government, have raised a spirit of inquiry to which the answer is obvious—a spirit favorable to improvement and change. Still, as peace alone can be a boon to a country situated as is Cuba, no rightly judging reformer can desire any but a peaceful change. I will, most probably, shake hands with you before another moon passes over. Until then, adieu!"

On Sunday, March 4, we bid adieu to Cuba, under great obligations for returning health, and, with an hundred others, we placed ourselves under the stars and stripes that float from the De Soto. Having passed the Moro, we were soon on our way over the ocean to the great river, where were deposited the remains of the discoverer whose name is attached to our excellent steamer. A swell, soon after leaving port, caused a rolling of the billows, and many of our company, instead of a fine dinner, had to take to their pillows, and rest quietly, with only a dry roll.

11

The morning, however, roused all hands to enjoy a delightful temperature on deck, and a smooth sea, and the breakfast table was well attended. A pleasant day was passed, in watching the sails of the tiny Portuguese men-of-war, as they drifted by us in almost a regiment, and the gambols of a school of porpoises, which were fishing in our vicinity. In forty-eight hours, we entered the muddy waters of the Mississippi, and soon passed its narrow bar. The river was alive with vessels of various classes, in tow of steamers, and its low, sedgy banks, destitute of vegetation and foliage, presented a solemn contrast to the beautiful verdure and ornamental grandeur of scenery of the "ever faithful isle."

As we progressed upwards, we soon came in sight of numerous sugar estates, whose neatness of culture, regularity and order of arrangement of the several buildings and dwellings of the owners, presented pictures of practical knowledge and business habits, far exceeding anything of the kind in Cuba. By a brilliant full moon, in a cloudless sky, the gallant De Soto bore us proudly and swiftly to the great commercial emporium of the South-west, where we arrived too late to receive the custom-house officials. Crowds of vessels were constantly passing, outward bound, laden' with the "staple of the world," of which, it is said, New Orleans alone ships 2,000,000 bales this year. The crop now is estimated as exceeding 4,000,000 bales.

CHAPTER XVI.

"—— Oft before my sight arise
Your sky-like seas and sea-like skies."

In connection with our visit to Cuba, as we
were prevented visiting Nassau, we supply our
failure to do so with the following very interesting and graphic letter from a valued friend:

LA GRANDE ANTILLA, April 30, 1860.

MY DEAR X: Rendered almost inconsolable
by the absence of your excellent society, and
our health having by no means improved under
the course of fast living we had been subjected
to in the '*La Siempre fiel*' city of Havana, we
determined to take a trip to Nassau, New Providence, and enjoy a few weeks' quiet rustication
among the 'Conchs.' Accordingly, on the —
ultimo, we took leave of their Excellencies the
Governor General and his beautiful Countess,
and bidding adieu to the frowning towers of the
'Moro,' found ourselves once more at sea, with a

fresh breeze, skimming gayly along in the direction of the Bahamas. As island after island
presented themselves to our view, we were filled
with admiration at their gem-like appearance,
covered with a never-fading verdure peculiar to
the Tropics and surrounded by the most placid of
seas, they looked more like 'floating gardens'
than aught else I can compare them to; indeed,
it required but a very little stretch of imagina-
tion to suppose that they were expressly designed
as a charming retreat for the goddess Venus herself. We were never tired gazing at them, and
could not but picture in our minds what emotions of delight their discovery must have
produced in the hearts of the illustrious Genoese
and his intrepid crew.

Disembarking at 'San Salvador,' we trod the
classic beach of 'Columbus Bay.' A day or two
later, we sought refuge from a squall at Harbor
Island, and, after enjoying the hospitality of a
noble old planter at Eleuthera, the prow of our
trim little yacht was turned towards the Capital
of New Providence. Delighted as we had been
with our cruise among those interesting islands,
the beauty of which I lack words to describe, we

were still more charmed with the appearance Nassau presented from the sea, as we approached the shore. It wanted a little over one hour for sun-set; it had been raining, but the squall had passed off, leaving in the western sky a few dark clouds, through which the sun's rays had success-fully struggled, to light up the town and country with shades and tints, the most brilliant we had ever beheld.

As we drew nearer, we perceived that Nassau was built upon the side of a hill, rising several hundred feet above the level of the sea, to which it fronts. The pilot, an active and apparently very intelligent colored man, took charge of us outside the bar, and shortly after-wards safely anchored us opposite a large, substantial iron building, which he informed us was the barracks. I must here premise that we strictly preserved our *incognito*, by representing ourselves to be down-east Yankees in search of freight. After receiving the official visits of the remarkably polite Harbor Master, and no less courteous Health Officer, who, *a la Espanol*, placed himself, or rather his services, at our '*disposicion*,' we prepared to go on shore.

We had been particularly struck during our cruise, with the extraordinarily translucent state of the water around these islands; as we moved up the harbor of Nassau, we distinctly saw beautiful colored fishes playing at hide and seek among mimic forests of coral, several fathoms below the surface. A rakish-looking brig, which we afterwards learnt was picked up on the coast of Cuba, whence she had been abandoned, having previously landed five hundred slaves, was laying at anchor in the stream.

We were put on shore at the Government Wharf, and having stopped a moment to admire 'en passant' the plain but commodious public buildings, we proceeded to the 'Royal Victoria Hotel,' where an excellent supper was soon got ready for us. Being somewhat fatigued, we retired early to our rooms, which were unusually large and airy, comfortably furnished, and, to our intense satisfaction, instead of a wretched Spanish 'catre,' which the poor C. had found so hard to get accustomed to at Havana, we enjoyed the luxury of a clean, wholesome, four-foot English bedstead, with mattress, &c., all complete.

You must know that the Royal Victoria
Hotel is under the immediate patronage of his
Excellency Governor Bailey, who takes a great
deal of interest in its welfare. The astute Governor, whose long experience in colonial affairs
makes him peculiarly well fitted for the position
he holds, on his arrival at Nassau, saw with
dismay that, unless something was done to check
the retrogressive condition of the town, it would
very soon go to the dogs. Hitherto, with the
exception of a few planters and merchants, the
Bahamians generally had subsisted by the mis-
fortunes of others; i. e., by wrecking.

Now, Governor Bailey saw at a glance that
Nassau enjoyed advantages of climate and
geographical position which, with a little
management, might make it as celebrated as
Madeira for invalids, and as popular as Newport
and Saratoga for pleasure-seekers in search of a
splendid climate during the winter. His first
step was to make the island comfortable.
Accordingly, he never ceased in his exertions
until he succeeded in having a first-class iron
screw steamer, the 'Karnak,' (commanded by
one of the finest sailors that ever trod the deck

of a ship,) placed on the route between New
York and Nassau; and as visitors began to flock
in great numbers to the latter place, he determined that suitable accommodation should be
provided for them. At his Excellency's suggestion, one of the largest and best situated houses
in Nassau was purchased, at the public expense,
and entrusted to the management of a competent
person from the United States. Every attention
was paid to the comfort of the guests, most of
whom, like General and Mrs. Pierce, came with
the intention of staying only a short time, but
were so well pleased, and derived so much
benefit from the climate, they resolved to remain
there all winter. During our stay, the fare was
exceedingly good. We got plenty of fresh fish,
poultry, eggs, mutton and beef, every variety of
fruit and vegetables, and *turtle soup every day!*

Governor Bailey's ideas in regard to drawing
visitors to the island (New Providence) having
turned out so well, and there being every prospect of a much larger number coming next
winter, his Excellency was prompted to apply
for a considerable sum of money to enlarge the
building, so as to accommodate a hundred addi-

tional guests. But, as this was to be done at the public expense, of course it required the sanction of the Colonial Parliament.

The discussion on this *momentous* question came off soon after our arrival, and gladly accepting the polite invitation of a friend, we hastened to the '*Salle des Debats.*' Our curiosity was amply repaid, for we never witnessed a more amusing scene. The oratory, with very few exceptions, was extremely indifferent. The natives were easily distinguished by a sort of *patois*, peculiar to the British West India Islands—not unmusical to the ear, but strangely absurd to one not accustomed to it. Everybody spoke at once, and upon subjects entirely irrelevant of that in regard to which they had been convened together. Indeed, they appeared to think the occasion suitable for setting forth their individual grievances, rather than attending to the public welfare; and there was no end of skirmishing. One rather tall, gentlemanly-looking old man, told one honorable member that 'he was at liberty to say what he pleased; he should take no notice of his remarks, as he had already more than once shown the white feather!' No reply was made to this by the dark-complexioned personage to whom the above stinging observation was addressed, but it evidently quieted him for the rest of the evening.

We were becoming very tired of the evening's proceedings, when, to our delight, an honorable member—evidently, from his tongue, a canny Scotchman—got upon his legs and begged 'their worships' to have the goodness to inform him when they intended to go into discussion about the 'Hotel Enlargement Bill,' as, for his part, *he was sick and tired of listening to so much twaddle!* This broadside had the effect of bringing the members to a sense of their duty; and I am happy to say we left them voting in favor of the bill.

The houses of Nassau, with the exception, unfortunately, of a few in the front streets, are kept scrupulously neat and clean, and seem to be well adapted to the exigencies of the climate. They have fine broad galleries, enclosed with movable Venetian blinds, which serve as a sort of evening promenade for the occupants. Many of them have nicely cultivated plots of ground attached to them, and as trees abound in every yard, the town, from a short distance, has the appearance of being embowered in a huge garden. The streets might serve as a model for the New York City Council, so free are they from dirt and dust.

The island is garrisoned by black troops, who look remarkably well in their Zouave uniform. These men are commanded by white officers, whose gentlemanly and courteous bearing makes their presence in society desirable.

With regard to the climate, it is undoubtedly the most salubrious in the world. *Yellow fever is unknown here;* a delicious sea breeze prevails constantly, and the thermometer, in winter, averages about 75°.

People attain a great age in these islands; indeed, they appear never to grow old. Upon renewing my acquaintance with the excellent and highly esteemed Chief Justice, the Hon. Mr. Lees, who has presided over the tribunals of the Bahamas for upwards of thirty years, I was delighted to find that he looked as hale and hearty as he did when I met him and his family, years ago, at the house of the Spanish Ambassador, at Washington. The same also may be said of the talented Attorney General, who, with his charming lady and interesting family, looked as fresh as they did the day I had the pleasure of dining with them in London, during the sharp winter of 1853; and as for that elegant, accomplished and handsome lady, the Hon. Mrs. John P——, why, she positively looks as young and sprightly as she did twenty years ago, at ——, in Leicestershire; but in regard to her they do say that she discovered the secret of that wonderful elixir, 'Balsam,' presented to the Countess DuBarry, to retard the ravages of age. However, dear X, should any of your friends go to Nassau next winter, and require medical assistance, they will find several eminent physicians there. The only names I remember at this moment are those of Drs. Chipman and Black.

Count Roval has gone to spend a few weeks in the interior of Cuba with his friend, the Márquis of V., and I propose departing for France very soon. *Tu amigo,*　　　***.

CHAPTER XVII.

"A physician should consider his obligations to his profession and society undischarged, who has not attempted to lessen the number of incurable diseases. This is my apology for attempting to make CONSUMPTION the object of a medical inquiry."

DR. B. RUSH.

The fearful increase of pulmonary disease in the United States during the last ten years makes it extremely important that all prophylactic and therapeutic means for relief should be carefully considered and impressively urged. There was a time when it was considered necessarily fatal, but farther knowledge of the physiology of the vital functions and pathology of what are called specific diseases, give the assurance that in its incipiency consumption may be checked and removed, even with hereditary tendency. Why the latter should exist we know not—why special defects of constitution should be communicated to offspring, inviting particular disease or promoting its attacks, we know not— why one individual should be prone to have a particular organ affected and not another, our science does not enable us to understand. In medicine as in other branches of knowledge, we may well say with the poet:

"Felix, qui potuit rerum cognescere causas."

Facts we can appreciate, and results lead us to courses of practice, physical and medicative, calculated to advance our knowledge of therapeutic influences, and to prevent or modify the action of causes to us unknown. More careful and discriminating observation, assisted by the rapid advance of science, has greatly improved our knowledge of pathology, and immensely increased our preventive and curative treatment.

Various have been and are the theories in relation to tubercular disease of the lungs, and still more varied are the modes of proposed medication. It is not my purpose to consider more than the fact which wide experience has settled, that the tubercular secretion in its incipiency may be checked, and its deposit in the lungs removed, by means calculated to invigorate the system and improve the vital forces.

My friend and preceptor, the venerable Professor Samuel Jackson, from microscopic examination of an incipient tubercle, has declared that it is an abortive or imperfectly developed cell which has lost its vitality—whether this be so, or the tubercular deposit an exudation from impure or vitiated blood, the treatment required is the same. You must increase vital power—strengthen nervous force and improve nutrition, so that healthy blood can be formed to be sent into the various tissues to repair the waste which is constantly going on in the body.

The integrity of the vital functions depends on the proper discharge of the duties of nutrition, and the health and habitual regularity of action of the power of assimilation. There is a constant waste going on in the various organs and tissues by the absorption, excretion and removal of organic cells that have done their duty, become effete, and whose place is supplied by new cell substance sent to repair the loss. In the process of digestion and assimilation, if imperfect forms are thrown into the blood, they are not properly vitalized, and of course they are not prepared for the part assigned them in the reproduction of tissue and structure. Whether these cells, which have done their duty and died, are deposited and remain in the lungs from inability to be absorbed for removal, or whether the original new cell formation is defective, is not material. There evidently is deficient vital power in the system connected with their presence, which must be renovated.

The lungs play an important part in the depuration of the blood of superfluous and excrementitious carbon, and in conveying oxygen to that fluid, while in the chemistry of physiology there are other and very important influences effected. This action is going on incessantly from birth, and never ceases until death. It therefore is greatly important that the organs of imbibition should be sound. Changes in temperature as well as in the density of the air breathed affect the lungs. A rarified atmosphere expands them unpleasantly and dangerously, and a condensed air oppresses them.

Lavoisier and Seguin say that an adult man

12

takes into his body, daily, 32½ oz. of oxygen.
According to this calculation, Liebig thinks four
days and five hours will be required to convert
the whole of the carbon of the blood into carbonic acid for exhalation. The chemists tell us
that this amount of oxygen is all thrown out
again in carbonic acid and water. If this be so,
and 32½ oz. of oxygen exhaust the blood of
carbon in four days and five hours, the amount
of nourishment to renew the carbon and keep up
the supply must be enough to reimburse 24 lbs.
of blood in that time. Liebig estimates the
necessity of an adult in ordinary exercise at
13.9 oz. of carbon daily. So it appears that a
change in the rarity or density of the air will
affect the general average, and the healthful or
disordered state of the lungs will influence the
result. These are matters suggestive of thought
as to pulmonary disease. At all seasons and in
all localities, in health, we take into the lungs
the same volume of air—its density, however,
varies. In warm climates we part with carbon
more slowly than in cold, hence the waste of the
body is slower in the former.

It is, however, not my purpose to present a

disquisition on physiology or chemistry, but simply to state a few propositions now commonly received, that may enable a general idea to be formed by every mind of the chief elements of treatment required to modify or remove causes of pulmonary disease.

Microscopic anatomy is contributing largely to the advancement of physiology and pathology, and chemistry also derives most essential aid from its investigations. A great stride is making in developing the uses and functions and modes of action of vital organs, and the progress of curative influences must follow improvement in such. knowledge. But my purpose was to state, that while a proper relation must exist between the nervous and vascular systems to keep the organism in regular healthful action, the basis of all vital power in the system is in the nutritive organs—of course including the assistance the blood has in perfecting its constituent globules from the action of the lungs. Whether or not nervous power be a secretion from the blood, or a mode of electric action, resulting from the union of two kinds of matter with moisture, is of no consequence in my present effort. Upon

the simple proposition here set forth, I am desirous of establishing a reasonable argument for
practical purposes.

In the rôle of the human economy, the nervous
power is essential to proper digestion, as the
experiments of Broughton and others show,
while its reproduction is equally dependent on
good digestion. While chemical forces are
incessantly acting within the body as without,
that action is modified by what we all understand as a *vis vitæ*. Of the nature of this, we
are ignorant, of its effects, we are cognizant.

"Causa latet, vis est notissima."

As we see an intimate connection between
nervous force and digestion, each so intimately
affected by the other as for us not to be able to
decide certainly which is the *primum mobile*,
so we have digestion essentially connected with
the integrity of the functions of the lungs, as
are the latter influenced by the proper discharge
of duty of the assimilative organs. The phe-
nomena of life are absorption of nutrition and
absorption of air—the oxygen of the air—
and upon these depend the support of the

animal organization. The influence of food and the influence of the atmosphere keep up health, and the relation between the two processes is natural and essential to healthful existence. On the other hand, *all diseases* may be said to depend on some internal and irritating impurity, whether it proceed primarily from the external world, as in infection, malaria, eating improper food, &c., or whether it be from a hidden vice of assimilation or excretion within the body and beyond the reach of our diagnosis.

In the treatment of disease, the all-important points are to get rid of and prevent the re-accu‧mulation of the morbid elements, (no matter how little we know of their minute nature, we do know their effects, and we often succeed in finding and opening channels for their happy elimination,) at the same time that the vital powers generally are supported by the remedies adapted to counteract the sure tendency to prostration.

I will not go into the investigation of the theories of consumption as to whether the de‧fective nutrition causes it, inducing bad blood, or whether the want of proper pulmonary action in not separating from the blood vitiated matter keeps in the system the injurious, if not the poisonous, influence of dead excreted material—the latter passing into the tissues which need vital reinforcement. It is sufficient for my purpose in thus glancing at the relations of the vital organs, barely to allude to existing conditions in order to bring to the mind the necessity for watching their action in relation to health.

The direct sedative influence of cold diminishes the action of the lungs, and, exerted over their large surface, enfeebles their vital power—this impedes their proper duty of oxygenation of the blood, which then, in circulating through the digestive organs, does not present the proper fluid for gastric secretion. So when the digestion is defective, the action of the lungs is influenced and obstructed.

Pulmonary disease,—I am not speaking of pulmonary disorder, of catarrh or bronchial irritation, which is readily curable by care—pulmonary disease, with tubercular development or consumption, is not always recognizable in its incipiency, but when you find wasting of the body, with paleness indicative of deficiency of red globules in the blood, with cough, quick breathing and quick pulse, you cannot go far wrong in taking up the treatment of the case as for incipient consumption. I make no reference to the stethoscopic sounds, recognizable by the experienced ear of the physician, as the object of this little volume is to draw the attention of persons, not medical, to the necessity of careful watchfulness of themselves. A great difficulty exists in this disease in discovering it early, as a special characteristic symptom is a delusive idea that there is nothing or very little the matter. Many a case of consumption progresses even to the end, by a steady and regular progress, where the patient cannot perceive that he is in the certain path to the grave. He thinks he will soon be well, and lacks only strength which is so gradually parted with that he cannot perceive it.

Experience has shown that it is almost only in its incipiency that consumption can be cured—it is therefore important to recognize its presence early and undertake its cure without delay. In phthisis there is diminished vitality, and increased irritability and tendency to inflammation in the intimate pulmonary structure—whether the latter is from the presence of dead tubercular matter or not, is not important—it is a fact, and we are called upon to soothe irritation while we brace up the general strength and promote absorption. This can only be done by attention to place the patient in an air less stimulating to the lungs by the amount of oxygen—less trying to the lungs and skin by a diminished and not variable temperature, and where, from diminished waste, less food is required for the support of the system, and the important tonic effects of exercise may be obtained without risk and without fatigue.

Experience shows that many, who in early life have exhibited symptoms of the presence of tubercles, have had their health improved and confirmed by a change from sedentary employment to active life in the open air—and dying of other diseases, post mortem examinations have exposed the marks in the lungs of the former existence of tubercles. It is not uncommon in families with hereditary predisposition to such disease, to observe cases of robust and perfect

health, even to advanced years, in those whose
occupation is in out-door business, with regular
exercise in all weathers, while others confined to
employments preventing the full enjoyment of
air and exercise, waste away and die at early
ages. Exposure to fresh air is essential to recovery in disease of the lungs, so that every in-
spiration shall present to the diseased organ the
vivifying influence of the pure element. What
Miss Florence Nightingale enjoins as the very
first canon of nursing, is the rule for enfeebled
and diseased lungs: *To keep the air the patient
breathes as pure as the external air, without
chilling him.* In acute cases requiring confine-
ment this may be done for a short time by the
strictest care and watchfulness, but as a rule in-
door artificial temperature does not realize what
the pure natural air of the external world has
the duty to effect. It is impossible to regulate
the temperature of a room and preserve the
proper density of the air free from adventitious
impurities from bodies around. A person with
diseased lungs should be only where the temperature of the surrounding atmosphere will
allow him to take exercise in it, and enjoy its

constant freshness.   This is an important axiom as a prophylactic in threatened cases, or as curative when disease is present.

It is a great mistake to shut up in the house weak and delicate subjects from the fear of taking cold—let them avoid sudden and serious changes of temperature, but with proper clothing remain in the fresh air as much as possible, and take exercise regularly, and, if possible, incidentally in business, and not as exercise. Pleasurable occupation in moderation, with incidental exercise in the fresh air, does more good in affections of the lungs, and in chronic disease generally, than the materia medica.   I would not undervalue the importance of certain drugs in the assistance they afford, which is often essential, but, as a general observation, I would remark, that in this disease quantities of medicines and mixtures of all kinds are taken into the system to a most injurious extent.   Judging from the notices of nostrums filling the public prints, one would suppose that there are hundreds of remedies for each disease.   It is worth while remembering what the celebrated Dr. Radcliffe said: that when he commenced practice he had twenty remedies for every disease, but he had not long practiced, before he found there were twenty diseases for which he had no remedy.

I have strong faith in medicine, but I have, in this disease especially, stronger faith in the *vis medicatrix naturæ*, which often has to struggle against the remedies administered, as well as against the disease. Medical science is advancing in power, but the facilities of procuring diplomas are so great that a crowd of unqualified men is annually admitted to the medical ranks, who impede and prejudice the true progress of correct principles. In no cases is this more apparent than in disease of the lungs, where the vital principle is constantly broken down by injudicious depletion, by inhalations, &c.; symptoms, and not the disease, being prescribed for. We have demulcents to soothe, and opiates to remove troublesome symptoms, but the cure is in the proper restoration of vital power to the nervous system, strength to the lungs and substance to the organic tissues; and this is to be done by improving the nutrition, increasing the assimilative power, making good rich blood and keeping it vitalized, which can only be done by proper food, plenty of air, and moderate, and in some cases, hard exercise.

The action of air, on the blood circulating in the lungs, as already stated, furnishes oxygen to combine with carbon, the chief depuration required, which causes waste, but during the process of actual combustion which here goes on, the heat of the body is generated. That heat is generated in the passage of fluid into solid matter is no doubt true, but the chief source of the heat of the body is in the lungs, where oxygen is combined with carbon. In warm-blooded animals the process is quick, in cold-blooded animals it is slower, but a fat, hibernating animal becomes poor by spring from this very combustion. A fat hog, shut up without food, will exist for several weeks, from its living on its fat, which furnishes the lungs with the carbon that the usual amount of oxygen respired requires, the waste going on without any increment of nutrition. This is the case with consumptives—the action of the lungs exhausts the carbon of the blood, while the nutritive function does not supply an amount of nutrition necessary to overcome the waste through that source. In this estimate no notice is taken of the amount of loss to the system of vital power by depletion, in loss of blood, poor diet, and relaxing remedies.

It would require a volume to treat this subject fully. I can only give the general idea, which I desire to impress on persons in weak health— spare and nourish the vital fluid—there is no such thing as general inflammation—you can have local inflammation, with general irritability, but you cannot have general inflammation. Depletion of the general system to relieve such a supposed state, increases general irritability and actual debility, and local inflammation, treated by general depletion, costs too much in the expenditure of vital power, so much needed for the' support of the system. General vital power is needed for overcoming local disease, whether inflammatory or only passively congestive, and nothing shows this so forcibly as where local affections arise in typhoid fever. Here you have local congestions and inflammations in a sinking state of the system, where general vital power is necessary to overcome such conditions, which are aggravated by any depletion.

The important idea I would impress is, that good digestion and fresh air affording the pabulum of vital refreshment, are the essential means to be looked to for improvement of the general health in consumption, as the only hope of correcting and removing local disease.

CHAPTER XVIII.

"An observation of the circumstances which precede the disease, or its so called causes, clearly indicates imperfect digestion and assimilation as its true origin."—Dr. Bennett.

The object of the previous chapter has been to endeavor to impress upon the reader, that an imperfect digestion, with want of the proper vivifying influence of fresh air upon the blood, is part and parcel of the condition of the system leading to and developing tubercular disease of the lungs. To render digestion properly efficient, exercise in the open air is essential, and the locality most serviceable to the patient is in such an atmosphere as is not variable, so that it may be taken regularly. My object is more to direct attention to the general principle than to give any detail of symptoms or pathology, as to whether the cause of consumption is in abortive cells, or a molecular exudation from the blood, constituting tubercular matter.

While a student of medicine, in Philadelphia,

I was particularly struck with a paper of the then eminent Dr. Jos. Parish, on phthisis, which suggested the necessity of constant exercise in the open air, to improve the general health as the essential means of cure.* Having in my own family lost several brothers with the disease, and suspecting in my own case there might be a development of it, I was specially watchful of the lessons of experience in relation to it among the patriarchs of the profession. For several years I was confined to the Chemical Laboratory of the eminent Dr. Thomas Cooper, in the South Carolina College, and was weakened in health (with constant pain in the chest, needing cupping and blistering,) by close attention to my duties, and had usually to travel during the summer to renovate. Finding upon every visit to a mountain region, breathing its fresh air and exercising in it, that I was always improved, I determined to change my profession, and, in practice of medicine, seek by constant daily exercise, on horseback, the bracing in-

---

* See N. A. Med. and Surg. Journal, Vol. VIII., 1829, for this most valuable paper.

fluence of the fresh air on a constitution with a threat of breaking down. The result was a perfect restoration to health, and a continuance of it, with little to complain of, until last fall, a period of thirty years. The attack of last winter is the only serious one during the whole of that period.

In my practice I have always followed the suggestions of Dr. Parish, and my experience has accorded with his; believing that if a remedy were found for consumption, it would be one to give strength and vital force to the system.

Dr. Bennett of Edinburg, in 1845, made a series of observations on post mortem cases which led him to the conclusion, that the spontaneous arrestment of tubercle in its early stage occurred in the proportion of from one-fourth to one-third of all the individuals who die after the age of forty. He states the observations of Rogee and Boudet, made at the hospitals of the Salpetriere and Bicetre in Paris, as indicating the proportion amongst individuals above the age of seventy, as one-half and four-fifths.

13

These facts, with experience of medical treatment, have induced Dr. Bennett to state, that

"Phthisis, in its incipient stage, may be considered a very curable disease; indeed so much so, that cure is, as we have seen, spontaneously accomplished by nature, in a vast number of cases.

"So long as misery and poverty exist on the one hand, and dissipation and enervating luxuries on the other, so long will the causes be in operation which induce this terrible disease. But the means of checking and controlling it on a large scale must be sought, not in drugs, but in hygienic conditions, and the diffusion among medical men of that knowledge and skill requisite for detecting the existence of the disease in its early stages."

With the general proposition alluded to, the question then comes up as to the proper mode of renovating the nutritive and assimilative functions, which is to be done by proper food, assisted by fresh air. We can only give, in a general way, the convictions based upon facts, that

animal food chiefly is what is needed by the
defective digestion in this disease—oily and al-
buminous matters, and particularly cod-liver oil,
which is easily digested, are most important;
but milk, fat bacon, mutton, beef and poultry
are very good also. Ripe fruits, sugar and preserves, if digested without eructation, are valuable as furnishing carbon. Of vegetables, the
patient must select what he knows agrees best
with him; for truly,

> "Try all the bounties of this fertile globe,
> There is not such salutary food
> As suits with every stomach."

Some one has suggested *Paté de fois gras* as a
substitute for cod-liver oil to those who cannot
stomach the latter—if they find it easily di-
gestible it is well suited to their case. The
general rule is to take the most nourishing diet
that the stomach will bear.

As to drinks there is but little to be said. It
is fashionable now-a-days to drink whiskey, well
or sick—and corn-whiskey is the popular liquid.
Taken in moderation it assists digestion and
furnishes carbon to the lungs, while it gives an
agreeable and often necessary stimulus to the

circulation. Champagne, if pure, is the least
injurious of the white wines, though Sauterne, or
the finer Hocks, are admissible. Sherry and
Port are much prescribed, and are valuable
where a stronger wine is desired, but the light
wines are usually preferable. Each case, however, must be judiciously advised on this point.

In taking whiskey the quantity must be indicated by the feelings, but there is a little risk in
an occasional case, as to what moderation means.
Dr. Cooper used to tell a story of his lecturing
Dr. Priestley's gardener for drinking, when he
said he only took liquor in moderation, and
moderation couldn't hurt. "But what do you
call moderation?" said the doctor. "Please your
honor, sir, only a quart a day!"

Volumes have been written concerning
climate, and numerous references might be
given, but as to exercise all agree. Sir John
Pringle always found that in fixed camps there
was more sickness from inactivity than from
fatigue, and this is the generally received observation. But in no disease more than in consumption is this needed.

In relation to climate the most important consideration is to find one that is temperate and equable, such as will allow the patient to be always in the fresh air for exercise. The late eminent Dr. Samuel George Morton, in his volume on pulmonary consumption, collects a number of observations as to the proper winter residence for consumptives. After quoting various writers, he says:

" It is probable, after all, that the West India islands are the most suitable resort for the consumptive, although sufficient observations have not yet been made to allow of a fair comparison."

He mentions of Jamaica:

"The mean annual temperature in the shade is, in the lowlands, between 75 and 85°, and in the mountains between 60 and 75°. Perhaps no part of the world presents a more equable temperature; which is attributed to the sea-breeze during the day, and the land-breeze at night."

Dr. Morton says:

"Experience has amply proved, that a mixture of sea and land air, such as exists on all maritime situations, is unfavorable to delicate lungs; and especially where there is phthisis, or even a predisposition to it. This rule appears to be of nearly equal application in all countries; and the fact is probably, in a great measure, owing to the sudden and extreme changes in the atmosphere in such situations: for it has been observed, that several sea-bathing places in the south of England, which are protected from the north and east winds, are congenial to pulmonary invalids; while other places but a short distance off, and which are exposed to the winds in question, exert a decidedly noxious influence. The latter remark applies to nearly all the localities on our coast with which I am acquainted; indeed, north of Florida, I am not aware of a solitary exception. Even those consumptives who visit the bathing places of New Jersey in the summer season, are obviously injured by it."

Even Florida is not free from changes—the weather there being sometimes delightful, but often the reverse.

In the foregoing pages I have endeavored to exhibit to the reader my views of the importance of change of air in pulmonary disease, or when it is threatened—that change being to a temperate atmosphere which is equable, and where the patient may avoid as much as possible the risk of "taking cold." Whether nervous power and electricity are the same is unsettled, but every one knows how barometrical the weak nervous system is—how a norther or an east wind depresses the strength and feelings. To all debilitated persons changes of weather are most disagreeable and dangerous, and changes in the electricity of the air affect the body. "Taking cold" results from an alteration of nervous (electric?) action, affecting uncomfortably and injuriously the vital functions, altering the distribution of nervous influence, and of course influencing the circulation. The great and important object in changing air is to get to a locality where the fluctuations are but trifling. In 1858, I spent two days in Philadelphia, in July, with the thermometer at 96°—next day I went to New York, and that night the thermometer fell to 54°. I took cold, and had asthma fixed on me for six weeks.

My experience of the climate of Trinidad,

where I saw no one with a cold, but observed great improvement in persons affected with pulmonary symptoms, has induced me to throw before the public my experience and views. I trust they may assist some sufferers.

The value of that climate is chiefly in its equability and temperate character—and in a tropical region the waste of the system from the combustion of the lungs being small, less effort is required for the nutrition of weak organs, which will have a better chance of recovery than where full duty is required of them.

Besides the disease I have been occupied with, I may allude to others which call for special attention.

There is a prolific class of maladies resulting from the over exercise and abuse of what may be called the "go-ahead principle." It belongs to our country, and deserves a place in our nosology. In the older countries such incessant labor in pursuit of wealth, as is characteristic of our business men, is unknown. There certain hours are devoted to business, and then they retire and have rest and recreation, but with our merchants and other business men, and lawyers and doctors, the wear and tear of body and mind are incessant. Every hour for years is occupied, and the tension of the bow is so constant that often its fibres gradually separate and the elasticity is destroyed.

Physicians are constantly applied to by persons with symptoms of heart and head disease, neuralgia and debility, which are but the results of over work and over exercise of mind and body. Affections of the heart are the most common, where the organ has undergone steady and continuous effort for years to keep up the body engaged in business most exciting, and requiring incessant labor and occupation. Individuals expect to keep up this intense exertion until they acquire an indefinite fortune, and are anxious for their medical adviser to put them on a course that will either not interfere with business, or quickly enable them to return to it. They do not reflect that the strands of life are loosening, that the excitements they have been submitted to are liable to be followed by a natural and certain depression, the end of continued exercise of vital power used up, instead of being recuperated by the practice of moderation in all things. How common is it to see the best energy and most active intellect breaking down by exhaustion—resting a week or a month, or sometimes a season, and going back again to the depressing influences so certainly destructive of what vital force is left. We are accustomed to see these cases, and to meet daily with apoplexy and paralysis as results.

"How much of late years has paralysis increased," is a very common exclamation, and every one who passes fifty begins to look for it, but will never realize that his incessant mental and bodily exertion is predisposing him to it all the time. This class of cases is steadily increasing, and needs a treatment somewhat similar to that we have advised for consumption, with the difference that here rest and not hard exercise is most necessary—laying aside business, and traveling in a pleasant climate with nothing to do but to see and enjoy the beauties of nature and art, where excitement is very moderate, and only of such a character as to create pleasurable emotions without depressing any vital function.

No one can travel in a country of luxuriant landscapes, where nature is exuberant of mountain and valley and tree and flower, without being agreeably exhilarated. The clearness of the atmosphere is communicated to his ideas, the balmy air soothes and softens the asperity of ill health, and solid acquirement of vital power accumulating gently from pleasurable influences, repays him for any sacrifices of leaving home. The dull and moping are disenthralled from their lethargy, and the spirit of renovated health buoys up and restores the anxiously desired nervous force, and puts new life into the previously enervated system.

CHAPTER XIX.

DIRECTIONS FOR TRAVELERS.

The facilities for visiting Cuba are so great that opportunities occur almost weekly. Regular steamers leave New York and New Orleans every twenty days, touching at Havana. The British steamer *Karnak* leaves New York and Havana once a month, stopping for a few hours at Nassau, N. P., the seat of government of the Bahamas, where are a good hotel and a pleasant, mild and healthful climate, where our own language is spoken, and many inducements exist for a visit from the invalid. The passage from New York to Havana is $60; from Nassau to Havana, $15; and from New Orleans to Havana, $30. The steamers are all fine, and the fare excellent, with kind and special attention from the gentlemanly commanders and officers.

A regular steamer, the veteran *Isabel*, leaves Charleston, S. C., on the 4th and 19th of each month, and makes her trip in three days, and sometimes less. The passage money is $40. This fine steamer, under the command of the experienced and watchful Capt. Rollins, is so punctual in her arrival at Havana, that if she does not enter the harbor within an hour of her usual time, much anxiety is exhibited lest a broken wheel or shaft, or some such casualty detains her.

Before you leave the United States it is necessary to have a passport, which you may procure from the Secretary of State's office at Washington, if convenient, countersigned by a Spanish Consul, but one from a Spanish Consul in any American port is sufficient. If you have several of your family intending to keep together, you may include them in one passport, for which you pay two dollars, whether for one or more.

There is a law against colored servants landing on the island, but if you get the Spanish Consul to put your servant in the passport, you can pass him without being stopped; if he is not included, you must get an order from the Captain General, through your Consul stating the circumstances of the servant being a nurse, &c.

Passengers should remember the change of climate, requiring a change of clothing, and make their preparations accordingly, placing in their carpet-bags such changes as they require, as the trunks are usually sent below, and much difficulty exists in getting to them. The fact that the variation of climate is so little in a tropical region, where summer clothing is constantly worn, makes it important that proper provision should be made. White linen is commonly worn by residents, and is well suited to the ordinary temperature, but is rather expensive, as washing costs not less than $1.50 per dozen for any articles.

Invalids will do well to take with them a little basket, containing a bottle of fine brandy or whiskey for sickness, with a phial of laudanum and one of paregoric, one of hartshorn, a bottle of calcined magnesia and one of mustard. A spoon and silver cup or tumbler will be of great use in traveling, both at sea and on land, saving trouble and time. A small tin apparatus for heating water to make tea or coffee, with a bottle of alcohol and a pound or two of the best tea are also important. The drug stores, however, in Cuba are very good and well supplied, and alcohol and medicines may readily be had. Still, invalids would do well to be supplied by their own druggists. A small, well-stuffed pillow, and a thick comfort, with a blanket, should be strapped on every invalid's trunk, the value of which will be found very great, as in Cuba you sleep on cots without mattresses.

Rumors of robbers induce many to carry revolvers or pistols—this is contrary to law in the cities, and renders one liable to the chain-gang, but in the country they are allowed. While on the island we heard of no case requiring one to be armed.

When you reach Havana, if you have not engaged rooms by letter previously, you will soon find the agents of the prominent hotels on board your steamer. Select one of them, and give your baggage in charge to him, who will see it through the Custom-House; but it is proper that when you land you should give an eye to it, as explanations are often needed by the officials. Don't be ruffled at seeing the clerks turning up your nicely arranged packing, but bear it with a complacent smile. Your good temper has a good effect on the officer, and often "a fellow feeling makes us wondrous kind." A polite and frank expression that the contents of the trunk are only for private use, will often be met by an equally polite reply in the form of a chalk mark on the trunk without any examination.

Having passed your baggage, and having received from the chief officer your permit to remain three months on the island, or thirty days out of Havana* for $2.00, your agent provides you with a volante or carriage for the hotel, and your preliminary difficulties are over.

The principal hotels are Madame ALMY's, near the *Alameda*, which seems to be always full; Mrs. BREWER's *Hotel Cubano*, 27 *Teniente Rey;* LeGRAND's, opposite the *Campo Militar*, near the *Teatro de Tacon;* Mrs. ROBBINS' *Queen's Hotel;* Mrs. LAWRENCE, *Teniente Rey;* BUENA VISTA HOUSE, *Calle de Cuba*, and we ought to mention

---

* When your passport runs out you have it renewed by any captain of a *partido* for fifteen days, and pay 25 cents. If you are traveling *towards* Havana, you are seldom asked to show it. Ordinarily, when you enter a hotel, your host asks for it, and keeps it until you leave. If you propose to remain more than three months, you get a domiciliary passport.

"The Both World Hotel," *Calle San Ignacio.* There are also others, which can be found on enquiry. There is a good hotel kept on the Cerro, by Woolcut, which is quiet and retired, and very airy.

The *Hotel LeGrand,* outside the walls, has a restaurant, where you call for what you want, and have your meals at any hour. The sleeping apartments are not as comfortable as they might be, but the table is perhaps less exceptionable than that any where else. Domingo, the *fille de chambre,* is very polite, and the waiters attentive.

The prices vary from $4.25 per day to $2.50, and board may be had at even less, but $3.00 to $3.50 is mostly the charge in good hotels; at Trinidad, at the *Grande Antilla,* you pay $3.00; at Matanzas, at *Ensor's,* $3.50; and at Cardenas, at Mrs. Woodbury's, $3.50.

In such a warm climate, necessity requires provision for only a day, and rents are very high. Mrs. Almy pays $600 per month, and Mrs. Brewer $400, and this all the year round.

A difficulty exists in procuring small change, which makes it important for travelers to carry

14

with them a good supply to save them money and trouble. Fifty or an hundred dollars in dimes and half dimes can readily be used, and American quarters and halves pass only for twenty and forty cents. The currency of the country is in *onzas*, or ounces, (doubloons,) valued, the Spanish, at $17, and the Mexican at $16; $\frac{1}{2}$ onzas, $8.50; $\frac{1}{4}$ onzas, $4.25; $\frac{1}{8}$ onzas, 2.12\frac{1}{2}$; *pesos*, Spanish dollars; *pesetas*, 20 cents; *reales fuertes*, our old Spanish 12$\frac{1}{2}$ cent pieces; *reales sevillanos*, or *sincillas*, the Spanish 10 cent or our dimes; *medios*, the old Spanish 6 cent pieces, or our half dime.

The old Spanish quarter, if the columns are prominent, pass for 25 cents, but if effaced, only bring 20 cents. As the charge in a volante for riding to any part of the city of Havana is a *peseta*, two dimes will pay it, while an American quarter will only be taken as a *peseta*. As visitors part with much of their change to the *caleseros*, it is worth while to have the purse well filled with dimes. American gold dollars pass as such in Havana, but beyond the walls, and in the interior towns, they are at a discount.

Visitors who intend to remain some time in the island should be well supplied with Spanish gold, but should exchange it for American, if any be on hand, before leaving. The large amount of American dimes and half dimes in circulation in Cuba is very striking.

As there are persons connected with the hotels and railroads who speak English, there is little difficulty in getting along, and on excursions you can usually procure an interpreter from the hotel if no one of your party speaks Spanish. The railroads are well managed, and receipts for baggage given and the numbers carefully entered on a register, so you may feel at ease about your trunks while in their care. When you get possession of them keep your eyes on them until you deliver them to your hotel agent or the Express. This is very necessary, or they may disappear.

To visit the public institutions no permit is required, except to the *Moro*, the *Cabanos*, and the *Presidio*—for these you must apply to the American Consul, who procures the desired pass. You should apply the day before, so as to give time—the rule of the country is never to be in a hurry. "*No corre priesa.*"

A common proverb in Spanish is

> "El que se apresura se muere, el que no tam bien."
> "He who hurries himself will die—he who does not, all the same."

In Havana, the street volantes charge a *peseta* for a ride to any part of the city, whether for one or two persons—or 80 cents to $1 per hour, *if you make a bargain before hand*, and this you should always do, particularly if you go beyond the walls, or the calesero will fleece you. The better plan, if you expect to be absent some time, where you are not likely to meet volantes for return, is to go to the stable and make your bargain with the *Alquilador*, you may then depend on the arrangement. Usually they charge a quarter ounce, $4.25, for the afternoon or evening, one hour or five—but you may make your own agreement. If you make no bargain, you may expect to be overcharged, as in Northern communities. We know a case of a friend who took a volante in the morning without any agreement, and he kept it most of the day—he was charged an ounce, $17.

In purchasing at the stores, they usually ask you a larger price than what they expect to take, you should therefore be aware of this and offer less, and adhere to your offer. One-half is frequently taken of the asking price. We purchased some lithographs of *ingenios* and views of the island at $1 each, and upon mentioning it to a friend, found that she had bought the same from the same place at 20 cents each.

Visitors to Cuba should provide themselves with something extra in their financial calculations (which should be very liberal), for extras will be found a heavy item even with the utmost watchfulness. As everything is very dear in Cuba, a well-filled purse is the greatest necessity to the traveler. It is very pleasant to ride on the pacing ponies, which abound, but nowhere else is the cost of equestrian enjoyment greater.

There is one suggestion to the visitor of very great interest, viz: to procure letters to planters, owners of estates in the country, or to resident citizens. There are exceptions, but letters from business men to business men, merchants, bankers, &c., are of little value. Letters to private gentlemen or planters will give you a warm welcome, and enable you to see the country and enjoy its true hospitality, but Mr. Hogshead's letter to Mr. Muscovado, with a draft upon the latter, you will find appreciated for the premium and not for your acquaintance. We delivered two such letters, and found they did'nt pay for the walk to the counting house, so we threw a dozen others into the crystal waters. If you have letters to planters you will find the kindest treatment and an hospitality that will put you at ease. Still, with all the coldness of the merchant, you must have a letter to one to receive and forward your letters—this he will do because it is a matter of business.

www.ingramcontent.com/pod-product-compliance
Lightning Source LLC
Chambersburg PA
CBHW030114030726
47498CB00007B/2376